Storms of Hawthorn Hill

The Winds of Change and the Fury of Love

Laura Lee

1   Storms of Hawthorn Hill

Copyright © 2024 by Laura Lee

All rights reserved. No part of this book may be reproduced or transmitted in any form or by any means, electronic or mechanical, including photocopying, recording, or any information storage and retrieval system, without the prior written permission of the author, except for the use of brief quotations in a book review or scholarly journal.

For information, please contact:
info@Lauxonpublishing.com
www.Lauxonpublishing.com

Disclaimer:

The content in this book is for informational purposes only and is not intended as a substitute for professional advice. The author and publisher shall not be liable for any damages arising from the use or misuse of the information contained herein.

Table of Contents

Chapter 1: A Mysterious Arrival

The Shadows of Hawthorn Hill

Elena Hawthorne returns to her ancestral home after years away, greeted by the imposing figure of Hawthorn Hill, where whispers of her family's past linger in the winds.

Chapter 2: Secrets in the Walls

Echoes of the Past

Elena explores the estate and uncovers hidden letters and portraits that hint at her family's dark history, sparking her curiosity about her lineage.

Chapter 3: The Tempest Within

Stormy Revelations

As a fierce storm descends upon Hawthorn Hill, Elena's thoughts are consumed by her family's secrets, revealing her turbulent emotions about returning home.

Chapter 4: The Enigmatic Stranger

A Chance Encounter

Elena meets Nathaniel Grey, a brooding local artist, who captures her interest with his mysterious aura and his connection to the estate's past.

Chapter 5: Whispers in the Wind

Messages from Beyond

Elena begins to experience strange phenomena within the estate, leading her to believe that the spirits of her ancestors may be trying to communicate with her.

Chapter 6: A Forbidden Bond

The Flame Ignites

Elena and Nathaniel grow closer, sharing their dreams and fears under the stormy skies, igniting a passionate bond that neither can ignore.

Chapter 7: Shadows of Doubt

Truths Unveiled

Elena discovers troubling truths about Nathaniel's past, causing her to question whether their love can survive the weight of their families' histories.

Chapter 8: The Haunting Portrait

Reflections of Desire

While investigating an old portrait in the estate, Elena uncovers a haunting family secret that intertwines with her growing feelings for Nathaniel.

Chapter 9: A Love Tested

Crosswinds of Fate

The intensity of the storm mirrors the turmoil in Elena's heart as she grapples with her feelings for Nathaniel amid a series of misunderstandings.

Chapter 10: Stormy Confessions

The Breaking Point

In the midst of a tempest, Elena and Nathaniel confront their feelings, leading to a passionate confession that changes everything.

Chapter 11: Ghosts of Regret

Echoes of Loss

Elena is haunted by the memory of a family tragedy that occurred in the estate, deepening her resolve to uncover the truth about her family's past.

Chapter 12: The Forbidden Room

Secrets of the Heart

Elena stumbles upon a hidden room in the estate filled with relics of forbidden love, sparking a desire to learn more about her ancestors' passionate lives.

Chapter 13: The Storm Within

Battles of the Heart

As external storms rage, Elena battles her own feelings of love and fear, questioning whether she can trust Nathaniel and embrace her heart's longing.

Chapter 14: Love in the Shadows

A Growing Darkness

Elena and Nathaniel's relationship deepens, but shadows of jealousy and family obligations threaten to tear them apart.

Chapter 15: The Winter's Embrace

Frozen in Time

With winter's arrival, the estate transforms into a frozen wonderland, mirroring the chill between Elena and Nathaniel as they face their personal demons.

Chapter 16: Beneath the Surface

Hidden Currents

Elena's discoveries about her family lineage lead her to confront buried emotions and hidden desires that challenge her views on love.

Chapter 17: The Rebellion

Love's Defiance

Elena decides to defy her family's expectations by pursuing her feelings for Nathaniel, igniting a fierce passion that alters their destinies.

Chapter 18: The Cursed History

Legacies of the Past

Uncovering more about the estate's dark history, Elena learns of a curse that has plagued her family, threatening her budding romance.

Chapter 19: Heartbreak and Healing

The Calm After the Storm

After a devastating revelation drives a wedge between Elena and Nathaniel, she retreats into herself, grappling with heartbreak and longing.

Chapter 20: The Heart's Resurgence

Whispers of Hope

With the help of a wise old family friend, Elena begins to heal and find hope, rekindling her passion for art and the life she once envisioned.

Chapter 21: A Reunion of Souls

Fateful Encounters

Nathaniel returns to Hawthorn Hill, determined to win Elena back, as the winds of change swirl around them once more.

Chapter 22: Secrets Revealed

Unmasking the Truth

Elena and Nathaniel confront their fears, revealing secrets that could either bind them together or tear them apart forever.

Chapter 23: The Dance of Fate

Steps to Destiny

At a grand estate ball, Elena and Nathaniel's connection ignites once more amid the elegance and drama, but outside forces conspire to keep them apart.

Chapter 24: The Final Confrontation

Clash of Hearts

In a climactic confrontation, Elena faces her family's legacy head-on, standing up for her love for Nathaniel against all odds.

Chapter 25: Embracing the Storm

Love's Resilience

As another storm brews, Elena and Nathaniel decide to embrace their love, regardless of the challenges ahead.

Chapter 26: The Path to Redemption

Forging New Beginnings

Elena seeks to redeem her family's past while carving out a new future with Nathaniel, promising to break the cycle of heartache.

Chapter 27: The Last Echo

Endings and Beginnings

As they learn to forgive, the echoes of their families' mistakes begin to fade, allowing Elena and Nathaniel to envision a new beginning.

Chapter 28: Winds of Change

New Horizons

Elena and Nathaniel embark on a journey together, leaving the shadows of the past behind as they explore their future in the light of love.

Chapter 29: The Calm After the Storm

Serenity of the Heart

With the storms of Hawthorn Hill behind them, the couple finds peace in their love, transforming the estate into a sanctuary of joy.

Chapter 30: A Legacy of Love

The Eternal Bond

Elena and Nathaniel create a legacy of love at Hawthorn Hill, ensuring that the winds of change will always carry the promise of a brighter future.

Prologue

The Winds of Change

The skies above Hawthorn Hill churned ominously, dark clouds swirling like the troubled thoughts that plagued Elena Hawthorne as she stood at the edge of her ancestral estate. The ancient stone walls loomed before her, shrouded in mist and mystery, their shadows stretching across the grounds like specters of a forgotten past. A chill wind whispered through the trees, rustling the last of autumn's leaves, and she could almost hear the secrets they carried — secrets her family had buried deep within the soil of this land.

Returning to Yorkshire after years away, Elena felt as if she had stepped into a world suspended in time, a place where memories lingered like ghosts. The air was thick with nostalgia, mingling with the scent of damp earth and the faintest hint of something floral, the remnants of her mother's beloved garden, now overtaken by wild brambles. It was a bittersweet reminder of a life once filled with laughter and light, now eclipsed by sorrow and shadows.

With each step toward the grand entrance, her heart quickened, a mix of trepidation and longing gnawing at her insides. Hawthorn Hill was not merely a house; it was a repository of her lineage, a place where love had flourished and pain had festered. As the wind howled through the gables, she could almost hear the echo of her ancestors, their voices entwined in tales of passion and heartbreak. The stories of her family had always fascinated her, woven with threads of intrigue and despair, but now they beckoned her to uncover the truth.

Elena pushed open the heavy oak door, the creak of the hinges sounding like a sigh from the estate itself, welcoming her back to the world it had guarded so fiercely. The interior was as she remembered: grand yet melancholic, filled with the weight of history. Portraits of her forebears gazed down at her with eyes that seemed to hold secrets—of love lost, of betrayal, of choices made in the throes of desire.

As she wandered through the dimly lit corridors, memories flooded back—of laughter shared with her younger self, of late-night tales spun by her mother, of the warmth of family gatherings. Yet now, each room felt like a sanctuary of sorrow, the air thick with unspoken words. A tempest brewed outside, mirroring the storm that raged within her heart, and she could not help but wonder what awaited her in this place of echoes.

Then, as if the very winds conspired to unveil her fate, a figure emerged from the shadows of the drawing room. Nathaniel Grey, the enigmatic artist whose name was spoken in hushed tones throughout the village, stood before her, his presence both unsettling and electrifying. With stormy eyes that held a world of untold stories, he seemed to carry the weight of the estate's secrets on his shoulders, igniting a flicker of recognition within her soul.

In that moment, as lightning illuminated the sky and thunder rumbled like a distant drum, Elena felt the winds of change shift around her. The mysteries of Hawthorn Hill were calling, and she could no longer turn away. Drawn into a tempest of passion and longing, she sensed that the storms brewing outside were merely a prelude to the turmoil that lay ahead—a fury of love that would challenge her very essence and alter the course of her destiny forever.

The winds whispered her name, a reminder that she was home, but also a warning that the path ahead would be fraught with shadows and light, secrets and revelations, heartache and joy. And so began the saga of **Hawthorn Hill,** where the storm of love would rage against the backdrop of a hauntingly beautiful estate, forever entwining the fates of those who dared to cross its threshold.

13 Storms of Hawthorn Hill

1

A Mysterious Arrival
The Shadows of Hawthorn Hill

Elena Hawthorne stood at the end of the winding, gravel-dusted road, her breath caught in her throat as she took in the sight before her. Hawthorn Hill rose majestically against the grey Yorkshire sky, an imposing silhouette framed by dark, swirling clouds that threatened rain. The estate, with its towering spires and ivy-clad walls, loomed like a fortress guarding the secrets of generations. The air was thick with the scent of damp earth and impending storms, wrapping around her like a shroud.

It had been years since she last set foot on this land, a decade spent chasing dreams in the bustling chaos of London, far from the whispers of her family's past. But now, summoned back by the weight of a legacy she could no longer ignore, she felt both a sense of dread and an undeniable pull toward the estate that had shaped her identity. With each step closer, memories flooded her mind:

echoes of laughter, the warmth of summer afternoons spent in the gardens, and the haunting shadows that danced along the walls when the storms rolled in.

As she approached the grand entrance, a chill wind swept through the trees, rustling the leaves and sending a shiver down her spine. It felt as if the very essence of Hawthorn Hill was awakening, eager to share its stories. Elena hesitated, her hand hovering over the heavy oak door, its surface worn smooth by countless generations of touch. A fleeting thought crossed her mind: what awaited her on the other side?

With a deep breath, she pushed the door open. It creaked ominously, announcing her arrival into the vast, dimly lit foyer. The air inside was heavy with the scent of polished wood and the faint traces of lavender that lingered from the days when her mother would fill the rooms with fresh blooms. Sunlight filtered through the tall windows, casting long shadows that danced across the floor, creating an ethereal atmosphere that enveloped her like a warm embrace.

Elena stepped inside, her heart pounding. The walls were lined with portraits of her ancestors, their gazes both regal and haunting, as if they were judging her return. The eyes of her great-grandmother, Eleanor Hawthorne, seemed to follow her, filled with a knowing sadness that stirred something deep within Elena's soul. She had spent countless hours as a child imagining the lives they had led, the secrets they had kept, and the love that had flourished and faltered within these very walls.

She moved through the foyer, her fingers trailing along the banister of the grand staircase, worn smooth by time and countless hands. The once vibrant colors of the tapestries had faded into muted tones, yet they still whispered stories of love and loss, of triumph and tragedy. Each step deeper into the heart of the estate felt like a step back in time, pulling her into the shadows of her family's history.

A soft rustle broke her reverie, pulling her gaze to a figure at the far end of the room. An elderly woman, dressed in a simple yet elegant gown, appeared in the doorway of the drawing room, her expression both welcoming and wary. "Miss Elena," she said, her voice carrying a hint of nostalgia, "it's good to see you again."

"Mrs. Whitaker," Elena replied, her voice barely above a whisper. The housekeeper had been a fixture in her childhood, a steadfast presence amid the shifting tides of family life. "I didn't know if you'd still be here."

"I could never leave Hawthorn Hill," Mrs. Whitaker said, her eyes glistening with unshed tears. "This place holds too many memories. I've been waiting for your return." Her gaze flicked to the portraits lining the walls, and Elena felt the weight of unspoken words settle heavily between them.

Elena's heart ached with the memories of her mother's passing, the last vestige of joy that had tethered her to this place. "It feels different," she said, searching for the right words. "Like it's been holding its breath."

Mrs. Whitaker nodded, her expression grave. "The winds have changed, Miss Elena. This house, it feels it too. There are shadows here—whispers of the past that have not yet been laid to rest."

A distant rumble of thunder echoed outside, sending a tremor through the glass panes. The clouds had thickened, casting an eerie light through the windows, and Elena felt a chill run down her spine. Perhaps the winds were warning her, signaling that this return would not be as simple as she had imagined.

"Will you show me the gardens?" Elena asked, needing to connect with something familiar, a remnant of her childhood amidst the uncertainty.

"Of course," Mrs. Whitaker replied, her voice softening as she led the way. "But remember, dear, the gardens hold their own secrets. They have seen much over the years."

As they stepped outside, the wind whipped around them, carrying with it the scent of rain and the distant sound of thunder. The gardens, once a vibrant tapestry of color, now lay in a state of wild disarray, as if nature had claimed them in the absence of their caretaker. Overgrown hedges and tangled vines obscured the path, but even in their wildness, the gardens held an untamed beauty that captivated Elena.

With every step deeper into the untamed wilderness, she felt a connection to her past—an energy that pulsed through the very ground beneath her feet. She knelt beside a patch of wildflowers, brushing her fingers against their delicate petals. Memories flooded back: her mother's laughter, the joy of picking blooms for the dining table, the stories shared on warm summer evenings.

But there was something else lurking beneath the surface—a sense of urgency, a feeling that the shadows of Hawthorn Hill were watching, waiting for her to uncover the secrets they guarded. As the first drops of rain began to fall, she felt a shiver of anticipation and trepidation course through her.

A low rumble of thunder echoed across the sky as she rose to her feet, turning to look back at the estate, its silhouette stark against the darkening sky. The winds were changing, and she could sense that this homecoming was merely the beginning of a tempestuous journey—a journey that would challenge everything she thought she knew about love, family, and the very essence of who she was.

With the storm brewing overhead, Elena knew one thing for certain: the shadows of Hawthorn Hill held secrets, and she was determined to uncover them.

2

Secrets in the Walls Echoes of the Past

The storm rumbled ominously in the distance as Elena wandered through the dimly lit corridors of Hawthorn Hill. The air was heavy with a sense of expectancy, each room whispering its own secrets, beckoning her to explore further. She moved cautiously, her footsteps muted against the cool marble floors, the portraits of her ancestors looming overhead like silent guardians of a time long past.

Curiosity pulsed through her veins as she stepped into the library, a vast room filled with towering shelves of dusty tomes and forgotten histories. The scent of aged paper and leather mingled with the faint hint of mildew, an aroma that both intrigued and unsettled her. This was a place where stories thrived, where knowledge lay hidden within the pages of books that had not seen the light of day for years.

She brushed her fingers along the spines, pausing to examine a particularly ornate volume that caught her eye. Its gilded title—*The Chronicles of Hawthorne*—gleamed in the low light. As she pulled it from the shelf, dust motes danced in the air, illuminated by the faint beams of sunlight that filtered through the tall, narrow windows. The book felt heavy in her hands, not just from its physical weight but from the gravity of its contents.

Elena settled into an armchair by the fire, the chill of the storm seeping into the house. She opened the book and began to read, her heart racing as she uncovered tales of her ancestors—stories of love, betrayal, and heartache that had shaped her family for generations. The more she read, the more she felt connected to them, as if their experiences echoed within her own soul.

"Wickedness lurked within the shadows of Hawthorn Hill," one passage noted, "a curse borne of unyielding love and betrayal that would haunt the Hawthorne lineage for centuries." The words sent a shiver down her spine, as if the very walls were whispering their warnings to her.

As she delved deeper into the book, the sound of rain began to patter against the windows, matching the rhythm of her racing heart. She lost track of time, consumed by the stories of family struggles and hidden truths. Yet, one name stood out amongst the rest: Lady Isabella Hawthorne. Her tale was a dark one, filled with longing and desperation, and it resonated with Elena's own feelings of being trapped between the past and present.

Driven by a growing sense of urgency, she decided to search for more clues about Lady Isabella. Leaving the library, she wandered down a narrow corridor lined with portraits that seemed to watch her every move. Each face bore a unique expression, their eyes following her, reminding her that she was not alone in this exploration.

The corridor led her to a small room at the end, its door slightly ajar. Peering inside, she discovered a cozy sitting room adorned with faded floral wallpaper and a small writing desk cluttered with papers. The window overlooked the wild gardens, where the storm raged outside, transforming the landscape into a blur of greens and grays.

Elena stepped inside, feeling a magnetic pull toward the desk. She approached it slowly, her pulse quickening with anticipation. As she began to sift through the papers, her fingers brushed against something cool and metallic hidden beneath a stack of yellowed letters.

With a swift motion, she pulled it free—a delicate locket, intricately designed with swirling patterns etched into the surface. It was tarnished with age, yet its beauty was undeniable. As she opened it, a faded photograph of a woman stared back at her— Lady Isabella, with her cascading curls and hauntingly beautiful eyes that seemed to hold a world of sorrow.

Elena's breath caught in her throat. This was the woman whose story had captivated her heart and mind. The resemblance was uncanny; she felt an unexplainable connection to this long-lost relative. Lady Isabella's gaze was filled with longing and sadness, as if she were reaching out from the past, desperate to share her tale.

"Who were you, Isabella?" Elena murmured, tracing the contours of the locket with her fingertips. It felt warm against her skin, as if it carried the weight of her ancestor's emotions.

Flipping through the letters scattered across the desk, she discovered heartfelt correspondences addressed to Isabella, each one brimming with longing and despair. The ink had faded over the years, but the emotions leaped from the pages as if the writer had poured their very soul into each word. It became clear that Isabella had endured a love affair that had defied societal norms, one that ended tragically and left her family in shambles.

One letter, in particular, caught Elena's eye. It spoke of a secret rendezvous, a lover hidden in the shadows, and the sacrifices made for love. The words danced before her, igniting a fierce curiosity about the fate of Isabella and the legacy of heartache that had followed her family for generations.

Suddenly, the door creaked open, breaking Elena from her reverie. Mrs. Whitaker stood in the doorway, her expression a mix of surprise and concern. "Miss Elena, you must be cautious with the past," she cautioned, her voice soft yet firm. "There are shadows here that you may not understand."

Elena met her gaze, her heart racing with excitement and fear. "I found this," she said, holding out the locket and the letters. "Lady Isabella's story… it's so tragic. I need to know more."

Mrs. Whitaker stepped closer, her eyes narrowing as she examined the locket. "Isabella's tale is one that should remain buried," she warned. "The past has a way of intertwining with the present, and not all truths are meant to be unearthed."

"But it's my family's history," Elena insisted, a fire igniting within her. "I can't ignore it. I need to understand what happened."

Mrs. Whitaker sighed, a flicker of sadness crossing her features. "Be careful, dear. The winds of Hawthorn Hill carry more than just the past. They hold the weight of our choices, and the consequences can be far-reaching."

As Mrs. Whitaker turned to leave, Elena felt a mix of determination and apprehension well up inside her. The storm outside intensified, rattling the windows and sending a shiver through the old estate. Yet she could not shake the feeling that she was on the cusp of something significant, that uncovering Isabella's secrets would illuminate not only her family's dark history but also her own path forward.

With renewed resolve, Elena returned to the letters, her heart pounding in her chest. The walls of Hawthorn Hill held echoes of the past, and she was determined to listen, to unveil the hidden truths that lingered in the shadows. The winds howled outside, but within her, a fierce longing had ignited—a desire to uncover the secrets that had shaped her lineage and to finally understand the depths of love and loss that bound her to Isabella Hawthorne.

3

The Tempest Within
Stormy Revelations

The wind howled through the towering trees surrounding Hawthorn Hill, shaking the very foundations of the estate as if nature itself were mourning the stories buried within its walls. The storm, fierce and unyielding, mirrored the turmoil brewing inside Elena Hawthorne's heart. She stood at the window of her childhood room, her fingers tracing the condensation on the glass as she watched the rain lash against the panes like a thousand tiny fists, desperate to break through.

The storm's fury resonated with her own emotions—confusion, longing, and a profound sense of displacement. Hawthorn Hill was both home and stranger, a labyrinth of memories tinged with joy and pain. She had returned seeking solace and understanding, yet found herself enveloped in an atmosphere thick with secrets and shadows. The echoes of her ancestors reverberated through the hallways, each one whispering stories she was only beginning to comprehend.

Elena turned away from the window, the darkness outside swallowing the fading light. The flickering candle on her bedside table cast dancing shadows that seemed to mock her sense of belonging. The locket and letters lay on the desk, an unsettling reminder of the unresolved mysteries that awaited her. She could feel Isabella's presence lingering in the air, a ghostly echo of a love story that had played out in secrecy, and she couldn't shake the feeling that it had somehow entwined with her own destiny.

"What am I doing here?" she murmured to herself, pacing the room. "Why did I come back?"

The memories swirled around her like the storm outside—her mother's laughter ringing in the garden, her father's stern yet loving gaze, the warmth of family gatherings that had once filled these walls. But those moments had been eclipsed by loss, the sharp pain of her mother's passing leaving a void that had driven her away to seek a new life, a new identity. Yet now, standing amid the remnants of her childhood, she felt as if the very walls of Hawthorn Hill were pressing in on her, demanding answers she was not ready to confront.

As thunder rumbled ominously in the distance, Elena sank into the plush armchair by the fireplace, its warmth beckoning her like a long-lost friend. She picked up the locket again, feeling its weight in her palm, and opened it, staring at Isabella's photograph. "What happened to you?" she whispered, yearning for a connection, a bridge between their two lives separated by time and tragedy.

She recalled Mrs. Whitaker's warning about digging too deep, but the pull was irresistible. A surge of anger welled up inside her as she thought of the shadows that had haunted her family for generations. Why had her mother never spoken of Isabella? Why had she kept those letters hidden? It was as if the very act of unveiling the truth threatened to unravel the fragile tapestry of their family.

Outside, the storm intensified, a violent clash of wind and rain that rattled the windowpanes. The sound was deafening, yet it oddly soothed her, drowning out her chaotic thoughts and creating a sanctuary of noise. It felt as if the storm were urging her to unleash her emotions, to confront the tempest within her soul.

Elena closed her eyes, allowing the rhythm of the storm to envelop her. The wind seemed to whisper her name, echoing the yearning in her heart. She felt trapped between two worlds—the past that clung to her like a ghost and the future she had tried to carve out in the city, a life of independence and ambition. Yet now, here in this moody estate, she sensed the inextricable pull of her lineage, the gravitational force of family ties that refused to loosen their hold.

"What if I'm meant to uncover this?" she pondered aloud, her voice barely rising above the roar of the storm. "What if my return is not just a coincidence, but a calling?"

A flicker of resolve surged within her. She had always been drawn to the stories of her ancestors, but now she realized they were more than mere tales; they were threads of her own identity. If she wanted to understand who she was, she had to confront the shadows that lingered in the corners of Hawthorn Hill.

Just then, a brilliant flash of lightning illuminated the room, casting everything into stark relief for a fleeting moment. In that instant, she saw her reflection in the mirror across the room—a woman standing at the crossroads of her destiny, caught between the past and the present. The storm outside mirrored her inner chaos, both frightening and exhilarating, and she felt a deep sense of connection to the fury that raged within and without.

"I will find the truth," Elena declared, her voice steadier now, resonating with the resolve of generations past. "I owe it to Isabella, to my mother, and to myself."

As the thunder cracked overhead, she felt an unexpected sense of clarity washing over her. The storm was not merely a tumult of nature; it was a herald of change. And with each roar of the elements, she sensed a transformation taking place within her—a shedding of old skins, an embracing of the unknown.

With newfound determination, she stood, her heart racing as she reached for the locket and the letters once more. Tonight, she would immerse herself in the stories they held. She would unravel the threads of her family's dark history, confront the love that had flourished in the shadows, and perhaps, in the process, uncover the true nature of her own heart.

As she began to read once more, the storm outside raged on, a fierce reminder that she was not merely a passive observer of her fate. She was a Hawthorne, and the winds of change were calling her home, demanding she take her rightful place in the legacy of love and loss that stretched far beyond the walls of Hawthorn Hill.

4

The Enigmatic Stranger
A Chance Encounter

The storm raged through the night, the wind howling like a restless spirit outside Hawthorn Hill. Thunder crackled ominously overhead, shaking the very foundation of the estate. As the hours passed, Elena found solace in the flickering candlelight of her room, her heart still racing from the revelations of her family's past. The locket and letters lay scattered before her, waiting for further exploration. Yet her mind drifted, as the echoes of thunder faded to the background.

The next morning, the storm had finally receded, leaving the world outside drenched and glistening beneath the pale light of dawn. Elena stepped onto the terrace, wrapped in her grandmother's shawl, the cool breeze brushing against her cheeks. The gardens looked wild and enchanting, drenched in shades of emerald and silver, the air crisp with the scent of wet earth and blooming flowers. Despite the chaotic night, there was a sense of renewal, a fresh start.

As she wandered into the gardens, Elena felt a strange pull to explore the surrounding woods, a vast expanse of twisted trees and thickets that bordered the estate. She had always loved the woods as a child, imagining them to be a realm of mystery and adventure. Today, they beckoned her like an old friend, inviting her to discover their secrets.

Elena followed a narrow path, her footsteps soft against the carpet of fallen leaves. The further she ventured, the more the trees enveloped her, their branches weaving a tapestry overhead that filtered the light into soft, dappled patterns on the forest floor. It was quiet here, save for the gentle rustling of leaves and the distant sound of a brook bubbling merrily nearby.

As she walked, her thoughts turned back to Isabella and the letters she had discovered. She felt a sense of urgency to learn more about her ancestor's tragic love story, yet the path forward felt uncertain. A chill ran through her as she considered Mrs. Whitaker's warnings about the past. Was she prepared for whatever truths lay hidden in her family's history?

Lost in her reverie, she stumbled upon a small clearing, where sunlight spilled onto the ground like molten gold. In the center stood a weathered stone bench, partially obscured by creeping vines. It felt like a hidden sanctuary, untouched by time. Just as she settled onto the bench, she heard the sound of footsteps approaching.

Elena looked up, startled to find a figure emerging from the shadows of the trees. A tall man stepped into the clearing, his presence commanding and yet shrouded in an air of mystery. He wore a dark coat that flapped gently in the breeze, and his tousled hair framed a striking face, accentuated by sharp features and intense eyes that seemed to hold a universe of secrets.

"Good morning," he said, his voice low and rich, laced with an accent that was unmistakably local. "I hope I'm not intruding."

Elena's breath caught in her throat. "No, not at all. I was just… exploring."

"Ah, a brave soul," he replied, a hint of a smile playing at the corners of his lips. "These woods can be treacherous, especially after a storm."

Elena studied him, captivated by the depth in his gaze. "I've always loved the woods. They feel... alive," she admitted, her heart racing. "I grew up here, but I've been away for some time."

"Then you must be Elena Hawthorne," he said, as if the name held weight. "Nathaniel Grey, at your service."

"The artist?" she asked, recalling the whispers she had heard in the village about a reclusive painter known for capturing the essence of the moors and the haunting beauty of the estate.

He nodded, a flicker of pride in his expression. "I suppose I am. I often find inspiration in these woods. There's a certain melancholy beauty that echoes the stories held within Hawthorn Hill."

Elena's curiosity piqued. "You know the estate?"

"Intimately," he replied, his gaze growing serious. "I've lived here all my life. The stories of the Hawthorne family are well-known in the village, and there's a particular fascination with Lady Isabella."

At the mention of Isabella, Elena felt a spark of connection. "You know about her?"

"Of course," Nathaniel said, stepping closer, his presence magnetic. "Her story has lingered like a shadow over this place. The love she shared, the pain it brought... it's a tale woven into the very fabric of Hawthorn Hill."

Elena's heart raced. "I've just begun to uncover it. The letters... they reveal so much but also leave me with so many questions."

He regarded her intently, his expression a mix of curiosity and empathy. "You're brave to delve into the past. Many choose to ignore it, but I believe it's the only way to find peace."

"Do you think it's possible to reconcile with the past?" Elena asked, her voice barely a whisper.

Nathaniel paused, his gaze drifting to the treetops swaying gently in the breeze. "I think the past shapes us, but it doesn't have to define us. Understanding it can set us free. But sometimes, the truth can be more painful than the silence."

Elena nodded, feeling the weight of his words. The shadows of her family's history loomed large, but Nathaniel's presence offered a glimmer of hope, a potential ally in her quest for answers.

As they stood there, a connection blossomed between them, charged with unspoken understanding. The air crackled with an electric tension, a mix of curiosity and attraction that left her breathless. There was something undeniably captivating about him—a brooding quality that spoke of passion and heartache, echoing the stories she had just begun to uncover.

"I'd like to see your work," Elena ventured, the words tumbling from her lips before she could think them through. "If you're willing to share."

A flicker of surprise crossed his face, quickly replaced by a warm smile. "I would be honored. My studio isn't far from here. I often escape to paint among the trees when the mood strikes."

"I'd love to accompany you," she replied, her pulse quickening at the thought of spending more time with this enigmatic stranger.

Nathaniel's eyes sparkled with mischief. "Very well. But I must warn you, my paintings often reflect the turmoil of the heart. You might find them... unsettling."

Elena felt a thrill run through her. "I'm not afraid of a little turmoil. In fact, I think I might be drawn to it."

With that, they began walking together, their footsteps blending with the soft rustle of leaves. The path twisted and turned, drawing them deeper into the woods, where sunlight danced through the branches overhead. As they ventured forth, Elena felt a mix of anticipation and uncertainty. Here was a man connected to the very essence of Hawthorn Hill, someone who understood the weight of its history and the beauty of its shadows.

But beneath her intrigue lay a nagging doubt. Could Nathaniel be trusted with the secrets she was beginning to unearth? Or would he, too, become another echo in the tempest of her family's past?

As the trees closed around them, a gentle breeze stirred, and for a moment, the world felt full of possibility—of answers waiting to be discovered and the promise of something deeper blossoming amidst the stormy revelations of their intertwined destinies.

5

Whispers in the Wind Messages from Beyond

The days that followed her chance encounter with Nathaniel Grey felt surreal, as if she had stepped into a painting—vivid and hauntingly beautiful, yet tinged with an undercurrent of mystery. They spent hours wandering the woods, where he shared his artistic visions, drawing inspiration from the landscapes and the lore of Hawthorn Hill. Their connection deepened with each shared secret, each unspoken desire lingering in the air like the scent of damp earth after the rain. Yet as Elena's heart opened to the possibility of love, a chill ran through the estate, sending tendrils of unease curling around her thoughts.

One evening, as twilight draped its velvety cloak over the world, Elena sat in the library, surrounded by the comforting scent of aged books and flickering candlelight. She had been attempting to piece together the fragments of Isabella's story, but an unsettling feeling gnawed at her, an impression that she was being watched. The air felt charged, electric with a presence she couldn't quite place.

Elena shivered, shaking off the sensation as she continued to read one of Isabella's letters, the words blurring slightly in the flickering light. Just as she was about to immerse herself in another passage, a sudden gust of wind swept through the room, extinguishing the candle flames and plunging her into darkness.

Heart racing, she fumbled for the matches on the desk, and as she struck one against the side of the box, its feeble light illuminated the room for a brief moment. She caught sight of a shadow flitting past the edge of her vision, prompting her to spin around, but there was nothing there—just the oppressive stillness of the old house.

"Just the wind," she whispered to herself, though the words did little to quell the unease pooling in her stomach. As she relit the candles, the flickering flames cast elongated shadows on the walls, creating an almost ethereal ambiance that made her skin prickle.

Later that night, she decided to retire early, seeking refuge in her room. The events of the day had left her drained, but as she lay beneath the weight of her grandmother's shawl, sleep eluded her. A restless energy filled the air, swirling around her like the whispers of the storm from days past. With her heart still racing, she closed her eyes and willed herself to sleep.

But sleep did not come. Instead, she was jolted awake by the soft sound of whispers, delicate and indistinct, fluttering around her like moths drawn to light. She sat up abruptly, her heart pounding in her chest. The room was dimly lit, shadows creeping across the walls as she strained to listen, desperate to decipher the words that seemed to dance just out of reach.

"Elena…"

The whisper floated through the air, clear yet ephemeral, as if carried by a gentle breeze. Her breath caught in her throat, and she peered into the dark corners of her room, searching for the source. "Who's there?" she called out, her voice trembling slightly, tinged with both fear and curiosity.

The response was a soft rustling, a sound like fabric brushing against skin, and the whispers continued, a chorus of voices intertwining. "Seek the truth… find the light…"

Elena's heart raced as she felt the presence of something ancient and powerful surrounding her. The hair on her arms stood on end, not from fear but from an inexplicable connection to the unseen world. The shadows in her room seemed to pulse with life, moving as if guided by an invisible force.

Gathering her courage, she swung her legs over the side of the bed and stood, her bare feet cool against the wooden floor. The whispers beckoned her, urging her to follow their call. She felt drawn to the door, which stood slightly ajar, as if inviting her into the unknown.

With a deep breath, Elena opened the door and stepped into the dim hallway, the candlelight from her room casting elongated shadows that danced across the walls. She felt an inexplicable urge to follow the sounds, to uncover the meaning behind the whispers that tugged at her heart.

She moved through the corridors of Hawthorn Hill, each step echoing in the silence, guided by the ethereal voices that seemed to lead her toward the heart of the estate. The atmosphere thickened, wrapping around her like a heavy cloak. As she approached the grand staircase, she paused at the top, the heavy air pressing against her chest.

"Elena..." The voice was clearer now, softer, yet insistent.

Following the sound, she descended the stairs, her pulse quickening as she neared the drawing room. The door creaked open slowly as if pushed by unseen hands. Inside, the room was bathed in the soft glow of the moonlight streaming through the tall windows, illuminating the space in a silvery hue.

She stepped inside, feeling the energy of the room shift as she crossed the threshold. The whispers crescendoed, a harmony of voices echoing off the walls, swirling around her like a tempest. In the center of the room, a dusty old piano sat, untouched for years. It was here that the voices converged, urging her to approach.

"Elena, play..."

The command was gentle yet firm, and as if possessed, she moved toward the piano. She sat on the worn bench, her fingers hovering over the keys. The moment she pressed down, a melody filled the room, soft and haunting, as if the very spirits of her ancestors were guiding her hands. The notes danced through the air, intertwining with the whispers, creating a symphony of longing and grief.

Tears pricked at her eyes as she played, feeling an overwhelming sense of connection to the past, a bridge between her heart and the souls who had walked these halls before her. Memories flooded her mind—her mother teaching her to play, the laughter of family gatherings, and the stories of love and heartache that shaped her lineage.

With each note, she felt the presence of Isabella and the generations that had come before her, their spirits alive in the music. The wind outside picked up, howling against the windows, but inside, there was a calmness, a sacred space where the past intertwined with the present.

As she finished the piece, the last note lingered in the air, resonating with a finality that filled the room with an almost palpable energy. The whispers faded, leaving behind a profound silence, but Elena knew she had made contact with something greater than herself—a connection to the legacy of love and loss that had shaped her family.

Breathless, she rose from the piano, her heart still racing. The whispers had quieted, but she felt a warmth enveloping her, a sense of peace washing over her. She had opened a door to her past, and in doing so, she had uncovered the first threads of a tapestry that had long been hidden from her view.

In the stillness of the room, Elena understood that she was not alone in her journey. The spirits of her ancestors were with her, guiding her through the shadows of Hawthorn Hill. And with each revelation, she would unravel the truth, piece by piece, until the legacy of love that had shaped her family was finally laid bare.

With renewed determination, she left the drawing room, ready to face whatever awaited her, knowing that the whispers of the past would continue to guide her forward.

6

A Forbidden Bond
The Flame Ignites

The days following Elena's ethereal encounter in the drawing room were marked by an intensity that seeped into every aspect of her life. The whispers of her ancestors lingered in her thoughts, entwined with the deepening connection she shared with Nathaniel Grey. Every time they met in the woods or shared conversations filled with laughter and shared dreams, Elena felt a flame igniting within her, fierce and undeniable.

One afternoon, as dark clouds gathered overhead, signaling the arrival of another storm, Nathaniel invited her to his studio. "I have something to show you," he said, his eyes glinting with excitement. The way he looked at her sent her heart racing, a warmth spreading through her despite the chill in the air.

As they walked through the woods, the atmosphere felt charged, anticipation crackling between them like static. The wind rustled the leaves, echoing their unspoken desires, and Elena felt the weight of her family's history slipping away, replaced by the thrill of the moment.

They reached Nathaniel's studio, a quaint structure nestled among the trees, with large windows that invited the wild beauty of the moors inside. The air was rich with the scent of oil paints and turpentine, and the walls were adorned with canvases—some finished, others in various stages of completion. Each painting seemed to tell a story, capturing the essence of the landscape and the emotion it inspired.

"This is where I come to lose myself," Nathaniel said, gesturing around him. "It's my sanctuary."

Elena stepped inside, taking in the creative chaos surrounding her. "It's beautiful," she breathed, her eyes drawn to a large canvas featuring a swirling storm over the moors. "You capture the wildness of this place so perfectly."

"It's a reflection of my heart," he replied, moving closer. "The tempest within is mirrored in the world around us."

Elena turned to face him, their proximity sending a thrill through her. "I feel that too," she admitted, her voice barely above a whisper. "There's something about this place... something that pulls me in."

Nathaniel stepped even closer, the intensity of his gaze making her breath hitch. "And what about me, Elena? What do you feel when you're with me?"

Her heart raced as their eyes locked, the world around them fading away. "I feel... alive," she confessed, her cheeks flushing. "I feel a connection that I can't explain."

He reached out, tucking a loose strand of hair behind her ear, his touch sending shivers down her spine. "You are a breath of fresh air in my life. You inspire me, Elena. More than you know."

The storm outside began to rumble, the first drops of rain pattering against the windows, echoing the tumultuous emotions swirling between them. Elena felt as if the storm were mirroring their own rising passions, the energy between them crackling like electricity in the air.

"Stay with me," Nathaniel murmured, his voice low and filled with longing. "Let's create something together. Let's share our dreams."

Elena's heart raced at the invitation, a part of her yearning to step into the warmth of his world, to blend their hearts and souls like colors on a canvas. "What do you want to create?" she asked, curiosity igniting her imagination.

"Something that captures this moment," he replied, glancing out at the encroaching storm. "Let's paint the emotions that stir within us. Let's give voice to the chaos and the beauty we feel."

She nodded, swept up in his enthusiasm. "I'd love that."

They gathered brushes and paint, and as Nathaniel set up a large canvas, Elena felt a flutter of excitement mixed with apprehension. They began to work side by side, the atmosphere electric as they splashed colors across the canvas, each stroke infused with the intensity of their connection.

As the rain began to fall harder, they moved closer together, sharing brushes and laughter, their fingers often brushing against one another. The storm raged outside, but inside, the studio felt like a sanctuary, a haven where their hearts could beat in unison.

"What do you dream of, Nathaniel?" Elena asked, glancing up from her work. The question hung in the air, an invitation to reveal the depths of his soul.

He paused, his gaze thoughtful as he considered her question. "I dream of creating art that resonates with people, that captures the raw emotions of life—the joy, the sorrow, the love. I want my paintings to tell stories that linger long after they've left the canvas."

Elena smiled, her heart swelling at the passion in his voice. "That's beautiful. I think art has the power to connect us, to bridge the gaps between our experiences."

He nodded, his gaze intense. "What about you? What do you dream of?"

She hesitated, her heart pounding in her chest. "I want to understand my family's history, to uncover the stories that have been lost in the shadows. But more than that, I want to find my place in this world—to create my own legacy."

As the rain continued to pour outside, they painted furiously, each stroke of the brush pulling them closer, weaving their dreams and fears into the fabric of their creation. The colors blended together, swirling into a chaotic yet harmonious representation of the storm that raged both inside and outside the studio.

Suddenly, the lights flickered, then went out, plunging them into darkness. A gasp escaped Elena's lips as she stumbled back, her heart racing. "Nathaniel?"

"I'm here," he said, his voice steady in the shadows. "Let's use this moment."

He reached for her hand, and as their fingers intertwined, an electric current surged between them. In the dim light of the moon filtering through the windows, she could see the determination in his eyes. "Let's embrace the chaos together."

With newfound resolve, they continued to paint, their movements guided by instinct and intuition. The rhythm of the storm matched the tempo of their hearts, each clap of thunder echoing the unspoken words hanging between them.

As they painted, the atmosphere shifted. The air grew heavy with tension, and Elena could feel the walls closing in around them. It was a heady mix of exhilaration and trepidation, the world outside fading into a blur of rain and wind as they lost themselves in their work and each other.

In that moment, as the storm raged on, they became a part of the tempest—a whirlwind of passion, creativity, and unspoken desire. The boundaries between them began to dissolve, and as Elena turned to Nathaniel, her breath caught in her throat. He was closer now, their faces mere inches apart, the heat radiating from him warming her despite the chill in the air.

"I want you to know," he said, his voice low and filled with intensity, "that you have awakened something in me, something I thought was lost forever."

Elena's heart swelled with emotion. "I feel it too," she whispered, her voice trembling. "You've shown me a world beyond the shadows."

In that moment, as thunder rumbled overhead, their lips met—a tentative brush that ignited into a passionate embrace. The kiss was electric, a melding of their spirits as they lost themselves in the storm outside, a tempest that mirrored the storm brewing within.

As they pulled away, breathless and wide-eyed, the world felt different, transformed by the fire that had ignited between them. They stood together, united by their dreams and fears, knowing that their bond had deepened beyond mere friendship. The storm may have raged outside, but in the sanctuary of Nathaniel's studio, they had found a spark of hope and love that would guide them through the darkness.

41 Storms of Hawthorn Hill

As the rain continued to fall, they returned to their canvas, painting not just with colors but with the essence of their souls, each stroke a testament to their growing connection. The wind howled outside, but inside, a different kind of storm brewed—one filled with passion, longing, and the undeniable pull of fate.

7

Shadows of Doubt
Truths Unveiled

The days following that fateful storm were both exhilarating and disconcerting for Elena. Each moment spent with Nathaniel was a dance of joy and discovery, their shared laughter echoing in the halls of Hawthorn Hill. Yet, beneath the surface of their blossoming romance lay a growing tension, a sense of impending revelation that lingered like a storm cloud on the horizon.

Elena was consumed with the memories of their passionate embrace and the vibrant canvas they had created together—a chaotic blend of swirling colors that mirrored the tumult within her heart. But as she moved through the estate, her mind often drifted to the stories of her family's past, stories laced with betrayal and heartache. Her thoughts returned, time and again, to Nathaniel's enigmatic nature and the secrets he kept.

One afternoon, as she explored the library in search of more letters from Isabella, a soft knock on the door startled her. She turned to find Nathaniel standing in the doorway, his expression unreadable.

"Elena," he said softly, his voice drawing her in. "I came to see you. Can we talk?"

Her heart raced at the sight of him, but a nagging feeling in the pit of her stomach warned her that their conversation might not be lighthearted. "Of course. Come in."

He stepped inside, closing the door behind him, the gentle click echoing ominously in the stillness. "I've been thinking a lot about what we talked about the other night—about sharing our dreams." His brow furrowed, his gaze drifting to the floor as he struggled to find the right words.

"What's on your mind?" Elena prompted, concern creeping into her voice.

Nathaniel took a deep breath, finally meeting her eyes. "There's something I need to tell you about my past. I haven't been completely honest, and I can't keep it from you any longer."

Her heart plummeted at his admission, and she felt the weight of his words settle heavily between them. "What is it?" she asked, trying to mask her rising anxiety.

He hesitated, his expression shadowed with conflict. "My family... they have a history with the Hawthornes. A dark history that I've tried to escape."

Elena's pulse quickened as she processed his words. "What do you mean? What happened?"

Nathaniel stepped closer, his voice barely above a whisper. "My father was a close friend of your grandfather. They were business partners in their youth. But when a deal went sour, it drove a wedge between them—one that led to anger and resentment. My family has been at odds with yours ever since."

Elena felt a chill run down her spine, memories of her mother's whispered warnings echoing in her mind. "But that was years ago. Why didn't you tell me sooner?"

"I didn't know how to bring it up," he confessed, his eyes darkening with regret. "I didn't want to tarnish what we have. I thought maybe if we could focus on the present, the past wouldn't matter."

"But it does matter!" Elena exclaimed, her heart racing as doubt crept into her mind. "Nathaniel, this changes everything."

He reached for her hand, desperation etched on his face. "Please, Elena. I care for you deeply. I don't want our families' histories to ruin what we've built together."

But the weight of his confession pressed heavily on her heart. She could feel the shadows of doubt creeping in, intertwining with the passionate bond they had forged. "What if they find out?" she asked, her voice trembling. "What if this ends in heartbreak? Can we truly escape our families' legacies?"

"Love is worth fighting for," he insisted, his voice resolute. "I believe we can rewrite our story, one that defies the past."

Elena gazed into his eyes, searching for reassurance but finding only uncertainty reflected back. The connection they shared felt precarious, and her thoughts spiraled back to the chilling history of Hawthorn Hill—the whispers of betrayal and loss that had haunted her family for generations.

"I want to believe that," she said, her voice barely above a whisper. "But the weight of our families' past is heavy, Nathaniel. What if it crushes us?"

His grip tightened around her hand, his warmth grounding her in the swirling storm of her emotions. "Then we will face it together. I won't let fear dictate our future. We can uncover the truth and decide what it means for us."

The sincerity in his eyes stirred something deep within her, but as she searched her heart, doubt lingered like a shadow. "But the truth can be devastating," she replied, her voice shaky. "What if we discover things that tear us apart?"

"We'll face it, no matter how painful," he said, determination etched in his features. "I won't run away from this. I care too much about you."

Elena felt a flicker of hope, yet the shadows of her family's past clung tightly to her. She withdrew her hand from his, needing a moment to breathe. "I need time to think," she said, the words feeling heavy on her tongue.

"I understand," he replied, stepping back, his eyes filled with an unspoken pain. "Just know that I'm here for you, no matter what you decide."

With that, he turned and left the library, leaving Elena alone with her swirling thoughts and the echo of his confession.

She sank into one of the plush armchairs, staring into the flickering flames of the fireplace. The warmth of the fire felt distant as she wrestled with the storm inside her. Memories of Nathaniel's laughter and the moments they had shared flooded her mind, but they were soon overshadowed by the weight of the truth he had unveiled.

Was their love strong enough to withstand the shadows of doubt? Could they truly defy their families' legacies?

As the night deepened, the wind outside howled against the windows, mirroring the tempest in her heart. Shadows danced along the walls, and she felt the weight of her ancestors' gazes upon her, urging her to uncover the truth—one that might either bring them closer together or tear them apart forever.

Elena closed her eyes, trying to silence the chaos in her mind. She knew that the path ahead would be fraught with challenges, but she also felt a fierce determination to discover the depths of Nathaniel's past and her own. The truth, whatever it may be, awaited her, and she could no longer hide from the shadows of doubt that loomed over their love.

Tomorrow would bring new revelations, and she resolved to confront whatever lay ahead, knowing that love was worth the struggle—if only she could find a way to embrace it without losing herself in the shadows.

8

The Haunting Portrait Reflections of Desire

Elena awoke the next morning with the remnants of Nathaniel's confession still swirling in her mind, a tempest of doubt and longing that refused to dissipate. She could feel the weight of the estate around her, each creak of the old house resonating with her turbulent emotions. The wind howled outside, its mournful cries echoing the turmoil in her heart.

Determined to gain clarity, she decided to explore Hawthorn Hill further, hoping to uncover more about her family's past. Perhaps the ghosts of her ancestors could provide the answers she sought, or at least give her the strength to confront the shadows that haunted her.

After a light breakfast, she made her way to the grand hallway, her eyes drawn to the array of portraits lining the walls—generations of Hawthornes gazing down at her, their expressions a mix of pride and melancholy. She paused before one particular painting, its colors dulled with age but still striking in its beauty. The subject was a woman, her dark hair cascading over her shoulders like a midnight waterfall, her deep green gown flowing gracefully around her. But it was the eyes—piercing and full of longing—that captivated Elena.

"Who are you?" she whispered, as if the woman could hear her. There was an undeniable connection, a spark of recognition that sent shivers down her spine. Something about the woman's expression felt hauntingly familiar, and she felt drawn to the portrait as if it were a portal to another time.

As she stood there, entranced, the winds outside picked up, rattling the windows and drawing her attention to the stormy sky. A sense of unease crept over her, yet she couldn't tear her gaze away from the painting. There was something about it that beckoned her to look deeper.

After a moment of contemplation, she decided to investigate further. "Maybe there's a hidden story behind you," she mused, her curiosity ignited. She stepped closer, examining the edges of the frame for any signs of secrets hidden away.

Her fingers traced the wood, and as she did, she noticed a faint indentation along the side. With a gentle push, she pressed against it, and to her surprise, the painting shifted slightly. Heart racing, she moved it aside, revealing a small compartment embedded in the wall.

With trembling fingers, she opened it, her breath hitching as she discovered a stack of old letters, tied together with a fraying ribbon. They appeared to be love letters, the handwriting elegant yet faded with time. Elena carefully untied the ribbon, her heart racing with anticipation as she unfolded the top letter.

The scent of aged paper filled her nostrils, and she began to read, her mind immersing itself in the words penned long ago.

My dearest Isabella,
Each moment without you feels like an eternity. The shadows of our families loom over us, threatening to tear us apart, yet my heart refuses to yield. I cannot deny the bond we share, one that

transcends the bitterness of our pasts. If only we could escape the expectations that bind us...

Elena's breath caught in her throat as she realized the letters were addressed to Isabella Hawthorne, her ancestor, and they were from a man named Edward Grey—the very name that echoed in the depths of her heart.

"Edward Grey," she whispered, the name sending a shockwave through her. It was Nathaniel's last name, the same family embroiled in the history of resentment against the Hawthornes.

As she read on, the letters revealed a passionate love affair between Isabella and Edward, a romance hidden away from the prying eyes of their families. Each letter was filled with declarations of love, longing, and despair, a testament to their desire to break free from the shackles of their lineage.

...I dream of a world where we can be together, free from the shadows of our families' past. If only we could find a way to escape...

The words resonated with Elena, echoing her own tumultuous feelings for Nathaniel. Was this forbidden love between their ancestors a harbinger of her own fate?

The deeper she delved into the letters, the more she understood the pain and sacrifice her ancestor had endured. Isabella's heartache mirrored Elena's own struggles, and the parallels between their lives began to intertwine with an eerie clarity.

In the last letter, she found a confession that sent chills down her spine.

...I fear for our future, dear Isabella. My father is aware of my affections for you and will do everything in his power to keep us

apart. I beg you, do not lose hope. Our love is worth fighting for, no matter the cost.

Elena's mind raced as she pieced together the implications of this revelation. The past was not merely a collection of memories; it was a living entity, shaping the present and future. The love story of Isabella and Edward had been doomed from the start, and now, here she stood, on the precipice of repeating their tragic tale.

Tears pricked at her eyes as she closed the letters, clutching them to her chest. She felt an overwhelming sense of connection to Isabella, and yet a surge of doubt washed over her. Would her love for Nathaniel mirror the tragedy of their ancestors? Could they escape the chains that bound them?

Just then, a soft knock on the door startled her. "Elena?" Nathaniel's voice called from the other side, filled with concern. "Are you in there?"

Elena quickly tucked the letters back into the hidden compartment, her heart racing. "Yes, just a moment!" she replied, trying to steady her breath.

As she opened the door, she was met with Nathaniel's worried gaze. "I was hoping to find you. I thought we could talk more about—"

She cut him off, her mind racing with thoughts of the letters and the revelations they contained. "Nathaniel, I found something... something important," she said, her voice trembling with urgency.

"What is it?" he asked, stepping inside and closing the door behind him.

Elena took a deep breath, summoning the courage to confront the shadows of their past. "I discovered letters from Isabella

Hawthorne to Edward Grey—your ancestor. They were in a hidden compartment behind a portrait."

His expression shifted, a mix of surprise and apprehension crossing his features. "What do they say?"

"They were in love," she confessed, her voice barely above a whisper. "They wrote about wanting to escape the constraints of their families, the same constraints that seem to bind us now."

Nathaniel's eyes darkened with emotion as he absorbed her words. "It's true. Our families' histories are tangled, but I don't want to repeat their mistakes."

Elena took a step back, uncertainty flooding her heart. "But what if we can't escape it, Nathaniel? What if we're destined to repeat their tragedy?"

His expression softened, and he reached for her hands, intertwining their fingers. "Then we fight against it. I refuse to let our love be dictated by the past. We can learn from them. We can be stronger."

As his warmth enveloped her, Elena felt the flicker of hope ignite within her. Perhaps their love could defy the shadows, that they could carve their own path, one filled with light and understanding.

But as she gazed into his eyes, the echoes of Isabella and Edward lingered in her heart, a haunting reminder of the price of love. Would they, too, find a way to transcend the legacies of their families? Or would the past ultimately claim them, ensnaring them in its relentless grip?

"I want to believe that," she said, her voice steadying. "I want to believe in us."

Nathaniel smiled, determination shining in his gaze. "Then let's uncover the truth together. Let's learn from their mistakes and forge our own destiny."

As they stood together in the dim light of the library, Elena felt a sense of clarity wash over her. The portrait of Isabella and the letters she had discovered were not just remnants of the past; they were a guide, a map leading her to the truth about love, sacrifice, and the power of choice.

With a shared resolve, they would explore the depths of their families' histories, uncovering the secrets that lay buried beneath the surface. Together, they would face the shadows, armed with the knowledge that love, though fraught with challenges, could also be a force for healing and redemption.

As they stepped out of the library hand in hand, the winds outside continued to howl, but within the walls of Hawthorn Hill, a new story was beginning to unfold—one that would challenge the legacies of the past and illuminate the path forward.

9

A Love Tested Crosswinds of Fate

The storm arrived with a ferocity that shook the very foundations of Hawthorn Hill. The wind howled through the trees, a haunting symphony that seemed to echo the turmoil in Elena's heart. Rain lashed against the windows, creating a rhythmic, mournful melody that matched her anxious thoughts.

Elena sat by the fireplace in the drawing room, the flickering flames casting dancing shadows on the walls. She cradled a cup of tea in her hands, its warmth offering little comfort as her mind churned with doubts. Nathaniel's words echoed in her ears: *We can learn from them. We can be stronger.*

But could they truly escape the shadows of their families? The haunting letters had opened a door to the past, and now, she felt the weight of it pressing heavily on her chest. Every time she thought of Isabella and Edward, she could feel the specter of tragedy looming over her.

As she gazed into the fire, she recalled the way Nathaniel had looked at her when she revealed the letters—his eyes filled with hope and determination. But doubts crept in, whispering insidious questions: What if their love was doomed from the start? What if their families' legacies were too powerful to overcome?

A loud crash of thunder pulled her from her reverie, and she set her cup down, rising to peer out of the window. The storm raged outside, rain pouring in torrents, obscuring the view of the garden. For a brief moment, she felt as if the tempest mirrored the chaos inside her, nature unleashing its fury just as her emotions churned wildly.

Just then, a knock sounded at the door, startling her. Her heart raced as she crossed the room, hopeful yet anxious. "Nathaniel?" she called out, opening the door.

He stood there, drenched and breathless, his hair plastered to his forehead. "Elena! I've been looking for you."

"What are you doing out in this weather?" she asked, her voice a mix of concern and relief.

"I needed to see you," he replied, stepping inside and shaking off the rain like a dog. "I've been thinking a lot about everything we talked about, and I wanted to clear the air."

Elena stepped back, allowing him to enter, her heart pounding in anticipation. "About what?"

"I know we have this connection," he began, his voice earnest. "But the letters... they've made me realize just how complicated our situation is. We need to talk about it."

Her stomach tightened. "You're right. But I'm worried, Nathaniel. The past is weighing on us. It's like a storm that won't pass."

He nodded, running a hand through his hair, water droplets flying off in all directions. "I understand, but I refuse to let our love be dictated by the ghosts of our families. I want to move forward with you."

The tension in the room was palpable as Elena wrestled with her emotions. "But how can we do that when we're so tied to the pain of the past? What if we're just setting ourselves up for heartache?"

"I don't believe that," he insisted, stepping closer, his eyes burning with intensity. "I believe we can create our own path, one that honors the love of our ancestors but doesn't bind us to their fate."

Elena wanted to believe him, to cast aside her doubts and embrace the hope he offered. But the wind howled outside, its voice rising to a crescendo, echoing the chaos in her heart. "It's not just about us, Nathaniel. What about our families? They won't let us be together without a fight."

His expression darkened. "Then we'll fight. We owe it to ourselves to try. Love is worth the struggle."

As they stood there, the storm raging around them, Elena felt an undeniable pull toward Nathaniel. Yet, fear and uncertainty gnawed at her. "But what if our love isn't enough? What if we end up hurting each other like our ancestors did?"

Just then, a loud crash of thunder shook the walls, causing them both to jump. The lights flickered, and the room was plunged into semi-darkness. A moment later, the candles flickered to life, casting eerie shadows along the walls.

"Maybe the storm is a sign," Nathaniel said, his voice low. "It reflects the turbulence we're feeling. But just like storms eventually pass, so can our doubts."

His words resonated deeply within her, igniting a flicker of hope. She moved closer to him, their gazes locked. "Do you really believe that?"

"I do," he said, his voice firm and unwavering. "I know it won't be easy, but I want to face whatever comes our way—with you."

Their faces were inches apart, and Elena felt a rush of warmth flood her heart. But just as she leaned in, ready to close the distance, a loud bang resonated from the window, startling them both.

"What was that?" Elena asked, stepping back, her heart racing.

Nathaniel turned toward the window, his brow furrowing. "I think something just hit the glass."

They both moved cautiously toward the window, peering out into the rain-soaked darkness. The wind howled, and through the torrential downpour, Elena thought she saw a figure darting through the shadows of the garden.

"Did you see that?" she gasped, gripping Nathaniel's arm tightly.

He nodded, concern etched across his face. "I did. It looked like someone—or something—was out there."

"Should we go check?" she asked, her pulse racing with both fear and curiosity.

"I think we should," he replied, determination in his eyes. "But let's be careful."

As they made their way to the front door, the wind howled louder, and the rain continued to lash against the estate, creating an ominous atmosphere that sent shivers down Elena's spine. She couldn't shake the feeling that the storm outside was merely a reflection of the tempest brewing between them.

Once outside, they squinted into the swirling rain, searching for any sign of movement. The garden was a chaotic mix of shadows and flickering lights from the house, but there was no sign of what they had seen.

"What if it was just a figment of our imagination?" Elena suggested, her voice laced with uncertainty.

Nathaniel shook his head. "I don't think so. There's something out here—something we need to find."

As they ventured deeper into the garden, lightning flashed overhead, illuminating a figure standing beneath an ancient oak tree. Elena's heart raced as she caught sight of the dark silhouette. "There! Do you see it?"

"Yes," Nathaniel replied, his voice tense. "Stay close to me."

The figure turned, revealing a familiar face, and Elena's heart sank as she recognized Nathaniel's brother, Thomas. He stood soaked to the bone, his expression a mix of anger and desperation.

"What are you doing here, Thomas?" Nathaniel called out, his voice laced with disbelief.

"I came to find you!" Thomas shouted over the roar of the storm. "You need to come back inside! It's not safe out here."

Elena glanced at Nathaniel, confusion swirling in her mind. "What's going on?"

"Stay back," Nathaniel warned, his tone protective. "You shouldn't be here, Thomas."

"I don't care!" Thomas shouted, taking a step closer. "You're risking everything for a Hawthorne! You don't understand what's at stake!"

Nathaniel's expression hardened. "She's not just a Hawthorne; she's someone I care about. You can't come between us, Thomas."

"But you're inviting disaster!" Thomas's voice rose with urgency. "Father will never accept this. You have to leave her behind before it's too late!"

Elena's heart raced as she absorbed the weight of Thomas's words. The storm raged around them, a chaotic backdrop to the confrontation unfolding before her. Confusion and fear swirled within her, mirroring the tempest outside.

"Nathaniel," she said, her voice trembling. "What does he mean?"

He turned to her, desperation in his eyes. "It's not true. I won't let anyone dictate who I love."

But Thomas stepped closer, his voice cutting through the wind. "You're playing with fire, brother. You think this is just a passing storm? The winds are shifting, and you'll be caught in the crossfire."

Elena felt her heart drop as doubt seeped in once more. Was their love truly worth the risk? The chaos outside intensified, mirroring the conflict between the brothers.

"I can't be a part of this," she said, stepping back, her voice laced with uncertainty. "If it means putting you at odds with your family... I won't be the cause of your pain."

"No!" Nathaniel shouted, his voice filled with anguish. "Don't say that! You're not the problem; my family is."

59 Storms of Hawthorn Hill

But the doubt had taken root in her heart, fueled by Thomas's words and the storm that raged around them. "I need to think," she said, her voice barely audible over the wind.

"Nathaniel, I…"

But before she could finish, another flash of lightning illuminated the garden, and she turned away, her heart racing.

The storm was testing their love, pushing them to the brink of despair. As she retreated into the shadows of the estate, she felt the weight of uncertainty press down on her. The crosswinds of fate were pulling them apart, and as much as she wanted to believe in their love, she couldn't ignore the storm brewing within her.

"Elena!" Nathaniel called out, but she couldn't turn back. Not now. She needed time to think, to understand the tempest raging both outside and within her heart.

As she slipped inside Hawthorn Hill, the echoes of their confrontation lingered in the air. The storm had not only unleashed the fury of nature but had also tested the very foundations of their love—a love now caught in a whirlwind of doubt and misunderstanding. Would they weather this storm together, or would it tear them apart forever?

61 Storms of Hawthorn Hill

10

Stormy Confessions
The Breaking Point

The winds howled outside Hawthorn Hill, a tempest that seemed determined to tear the world asunder. Rain lashed against the windows, creating a cacophony of sound that echoed the turmoil raging within Elena's heart. She paced the dimly lit corridor, her thoughts spiraling in a chaotic dance of doubt and longing.

The confrontation with Nathaniel's brother, Thomas, echoed in her mind. His warnings loomed large, painting a vivid picture of the dangers that lay ahead if she continued down this path with Nathaniel. Could their love withstand the pressure of familial expectations and the shadows of the past?

As she reached the drawing room, she stopped short, her breath catching in her throat. Nathaniel stood by the fireplace, his silhouette framed by the flickering flames, his expression one of deep contemplation. The sight of him stirred something deep within her—a yearning that ignited her very core.

"Elena," he said, his voice low and filled with urgency as he turned to face her. "We need to talk. Now."

The intensity in his gaze sent a shiver down her spine, a mix of fear and excitement that left her breathless. "I know," she replied, stepping forward. "I can't shake what Thomas said. It's all so overwhelming."

"I can't let him come between us," Nathaniel declared, his fists clenched at his sides. "This is about us, and I refuse to let anyone dictate my feelings."

"Easier said than done," she countered, a tremor in her voice. "What if he's right? What if our love is just a reckless storm that will leave us both broken in its wake?"

"No." He stepped closer, his expression fierce, determination radiating from him like heat from the fire. "Our love is not reckless. It's real, and it's worth fighting for."

Elena's heart raced at the raw intensity of his words. "But at what cost? I don't want to be the reason your family is torn apart."

He closed the distance between them, his voice dropping to a whisper. "You're not the reason. My family's expectations are. I've spent too long trying to live up to them, trying to fit into a mold that doesn't reflect who I am. But with you…everything changes."

The way he looked at her, with such sincerity and longing, melted away some of her doubts. "What if we fail? What if we end up hurt, just like Isabella and Edward?"

His eyes softened, a mixture of pain and hope glimmering in the depths. "That's the risk of love. But if we don't take that leap, we'll never know what could have been. We owe it to ourselves to try."

Tears stung her eyes as she fought against the whirlwind of emotions within her. The storm outside raged on, a reflection of her inner turmoil, but Nathaniel's presence grounded her. She could feel the pull of their connection, a bond that transcended the fears and doubts swirling around them.

"Please," he said, reaching out to cup her face in his hands. "Don't pull away from me. We can face this together. I want to be with you, no matter the obstacles."

The sincerity in his gaze broke through her defenses, and in that moment, she realized how much she wanted to believe in them, in the possibility of a love that could conquer all. "I want to be with you too," she confessed, her voice trembling. "But I'm terrified."

He smiled softly, his thumbs brushing away the tears that had escaped down her cheeks. "So am I. But fear shouldn't dictate our choices. Love is about vulnerability, about laying bare our hearts even when it feels risky."

Elena took a shaky breath, his words resonating within her like a fragile yet powerful truth. "You're right. I've been so focused on the past that I've forgotten to embrace what's in front of me."

Their eyes locked, and the air crackled with unspoken emotions. In that moment, everything else faded away—the storm, the past, the uncertainties. It was just the two of them, standing on the precipice of something beautiful and terrifying.

"I love you, Elena," Nathaniel said, his voice raw with emotion. "I've loved you since the moment we met, and nothing will change that."

The weight of his confession hung between them, heavy and electric. Elena's heart soared at his words, a rush of warmth flooding her veins. "I love you too, Nathaniel. I've been afraid to admit it, afraid of what it might mean for us. But I can't deny it anymore."

As the storm raged outside, the world felt impossibly small, and the space between them closed to a mere breath. Their hearts beat in synchrony, a rhythm fueled by the intensity of their feelings.

In a moment that felt suspended in time, Nathaniel leaned in, his lips brushing against hers with a tenderness that ignited a fire within her. The kiss was a sweet yet fervent promise, a declaration of their commitment to one another despite the chaos surrounding them.

Elena melted into him, her doubts dissipating like the clouds parting for the sun. With each heartbeat, she felt the weight of her fears lifting, replaced by a newfound clarity. She was ready to embrace the love that lay before her, ready to face whatever challenges awaited them.

As they pulled away, breathless and wide-eyed, Elena couldn't help but smile through her tears. "We'll fight for this, won't we?"

"Always," Nathaniel vowed, his hands still cradling her face. "No matter the storm, we'll stand together."

Outside, the winds howled in protest, but inside Hawthorn Hill, the tempest of their confessions had given way to a fierce resolve. Together, they would navigate the treacherous waters of their intertwined destinies, united by a love that burned brightly against the backdrop of uncertainty.

But as they stood together in that moment, Elena couldn't shake the feeling that the storm was far from over. The winds of change were just beginning to stir, and they would have to brace themselves for the challenges that lay ahead. Yet for the first time, she felt a flicker of hope—a belief that perhaps, just perhaps, they could weather the storm and emerge stronger on the other side.

11

Ghosts of Regret Echoes of Loss

The storm had finally begun to wane, leaving behind a somber stillness that blanketed Hawthorn Hill. Elena stood in the drawing room, gazing out at the remnants of the tempest—wet leaves strewn across the ground and branches swaying gently in the breeze. Yet, despite the calm that had settled in, an unsettling sense of foreboding clung to her, refusing to dissipate.

The kiss she and Nathaniel had shared still lingered on her lips, a beautiful promise amidst the chaos. But as she turned away from the window, the shadows of the past loomed large in her mind, and she could feel the weight of her family's history pressing down on her.

Elena's gaze fell upon the ornate mirror hanging above the fireplace, its surface reflecting the flickering candlelight. In its depths, she saw more than just her own image; she saw the faces of her ancestors, the sorrow etched into their features, their eyes filled with untold stories. Among them was Isabella, her great-grandmother, whose tragic fate had woven a dark thread through the fabric of the Hawthorne legacy.

She shivered, recalling the tales her mother had shared—the whispers of a night shrouded in darkness when Isabella had lost everything she held dear. The tragedy that unfolded on these very grounds had cast a long shadow over their family, one that Elena felt compelled to confront.

"What happened to you, Isabella?" she whispered, her voice barely audible above the soft crackling of the fireplace. "What ghosts haunt this estate?"

Determined to uncover the truth, she turned away from the mirror and ventured toward the library, where the musty scent of old books filled the air. It had always been her refuge, a place where she could escape into the worlds crafted by the authors of the past. Now, it felt like a sanctuary of secrets waiting to be unearthed.

As she pushed open the heavy oak door, the dim light flickered overhead, casting eerie shadows that danced across the walls. She ran her fingers along the spines of the books, searching for something that might illuminate the dark corners of her family's history. Finally, her hand landed on an old leather-bound journal, its cover worn and faded. She pulled it from the shelf, the weight of it feeling significant in her hands.

Settling into a nearby armchair, she opened the journal, its pages yellowed with age. As she began to read, the elegant script of her great-grandmother emerged before her eyes, filled with longing, despair, and fragmented memories.

Isabella's words poured forth, recounting the joy of her youth and the love she had for Edward, a love that had burned brightly until tragedy extinguished it. Each entry peeled back layers of the past, revealing the intricate tapestry of life at Hawthorn Hill, woven with threads of love and loss.

Then, one entry caught Elena's attention:

October 17, 1887. The day the storm came. I shall never forget the sound of the wind, the way it howled like a banshee through the halls. That night, everything changed. Edward and I had plans to elope, to leave this cursed estate behind, but fate had other ideas.

A chill ran down Elena's spine. She continued reading, her heart racing as Isabella detailed the events of that fateful night—how the tempest had unleashed chaos upon the estate, tearing apart the very fabric of their lives. The journal spoke of a betrayal, a dark secret hidden within the walls of Hawthorn Hill that had shattered Isabella's world, leaving her trapped in a cycle of grief.

I will never forgive myself for what happened. The echoes of that night haunt me still, shadows that will never fade. How can I move forward when the past refuses to let me go?

Elena's heart ached for her great-grandmother, for the weight of sorrow that had carried through generations. She couldn't help but wonder if Isabella's spirit lingered in the estate, trapped by the ghosts of her regret.

But with each word, the determination within Elena grew stronger. She needed to uncover the truth of that tragic night, to confront the darkness that had plagued her family for too long. If she didn't, she feared she would become another echo of loss, another ghost haunting the halls of Hawthorn Hill.

As she continued to read, the thunderous crash of lightning outside startled her, a sudden reminder of the storm that had once changed everything. In that moment, she knew she had to confront

Nathaniel. She needed to share what she had discovered, to invite him into her world of secrets and regrets.

Elena stood, clutching the journal to her chest, her resolve solidifying. She would not allow her family's past to dictate her future. With newfound purpose, she hurried through the winding corridors of the estate, the soft glow of the candles guiding her way.

When she reached Nathaniel's studio, she paused, her heart racing with anticipation and fear. She had shared her dreams and fears with him, but now she was about to expose the painful truth that haunted her family.

Taking a deep breath, she knocked softly on the door. "Nathaniel?"

"Come in," he called, his voice warm and inviting.

Pushing the door open, Elena found him surrounded by canvases, the air filled with the scent of oil paint and turpentine. He looked up, his eyes lighting up as he saw her. "Elena, you're back! I was just thinking about you."

"I've been reading," she said, her voice trembling with a mix of excitement and apprehension. "About Isabella. About the night everything changed."

Nathaniel's expression shifted, curiosity piquing in his eyes. "What did you find?"

She stepped closer, the journal still clutched in her hands. "There's so much pain tied to this place, Nathaniel. Isabella's words—they're filled with regret and sorrow. It's as if the estate itself is holding onto her grief."

He moved closer, taking the journal from her hands gently, his brows furrowing as he began to skim through the pages. "You think the past is still affecting us? That her spirit is lingering here?"

"I can't shake the feeling," she admitted, her voice low. "The more I read, the more I understand how deeply intertwined our lives are with the ghosts of our family. We need to uncover what happened that night—the betrayal that shattered her life. Only then can we break free from its hold."

Nathaniel looked up from the journal, his eyes intense and focused. "I'll help you, Elena. Whatever it takes. We'll confront the truth together."

Her heart swelled at his words, but a tinge of doubt remained. "But what if we find something we wish we hadn't? What if the truth is more painful than the ghosts we're trying to escape?"

He took her hands in his, grounding her in that moment. "Then we'll face it together. We owe it to Isabella and to ourselves to uncover the truth. It's the only way we can move forward."

Elena nodded, a sense of resolve washing over her. "Then let's begin. I won't let the ghosts of regret keep us trapped any longer."

As they stood together in the studio, the weight of the past loomed large, but the promise of discovery shimmered on the horizon. They would delve into the shadows, unearthing the truths that had haunted their families for generations. Together, they would confront the echoes of loss, not only for Isabella but for themselves, forging a path toward a future free from the burdens of their past.

As the final remnants of the storm faded into the distance, Elena felt a flicker of hope igniting within her. The winds of change were blowing, and with Nathaniel by her side, she was ready to embrace whatever lay ahead.

12

The Forbidden Room
Secrets of the Heart

The morning sun broke through the remnants of the storm, casting a warm glow over Hawthorn Hill. After a restless night spent poring over Isabella's journal with Nathaniel, Elena felt an electric anticipation thrumming in her veins. Today, she resolved to dig deeper into her family's history, to uncover the hidden stories that lay dormant within the estate's walls.

Fueled by determination, she decided to explore a part of the estate she had avoided—an old wing that had long been shuttered and left to the ravages of time. Rumors of a forbidden room lingered in the whispers of the housekeepers, tales of a space that had once been a sanctuary for those whose love was deemed unacceptable.

"Elena!" Nathaniel called, appearing in the hallway just as she was about to ascend the creaking staircase. "Where are you going?"

"I want to explore the north wing," she replied, excitement mingling with trepidation. "I've heard there's a room up there that holds secrets about our family's past."

His brow furrowed slightly. "The north wing? It hasn't been touched in years. It's said to be cursed, filled with memories that are better left undisturbed."

"Maybe so," she insisted, her heart racing at the thought of discovery. "But what if it holds the key to understanding who we are? I need to know."

Nathaniel hesitated, his eyes searching hers, but eventually he nodded. "All right, but I'm coming with you. I don't want you to face whatever's in there alone."

Together, they ascended the staircase, the floorboards groaning beneath their feet as they approached the door that separated them from the north wing. Elena felt a thrill of apprehension mixed with curiosity. What awaited them on the other side?

With a deep breath, she pushed open the heavy door, the hinges protesting in a sorrowful creak. The air was thick with dust and the scent of forgotten memories. Dim light filtered through the grime-covered windows, revealing a hallway lined with faded portraits and tattered wallpaper, remnants of a once-vibrant space.

As they stepped inside, the atmosphere shifted. It felt as though they were entering a realm frozen in time, a world untouched by the passing years. Cobwebs hung in the corners, and the faint scent of mildew hung in the air, but amidst the decay, Elena sensed a pulse of life, a whisper of the stories that had unfolded within these walls.

"What do you think we'll find?" Nathaniel asked, his voice barely above a whisper as they moved deeper into the wing.

"I don't know," Elena replied, her eyes scanning the surroundings. "But I feel like this place holds more than just dust and shadows."

They wandered through the narrow hallways, passing door after door, each one a portal to the past. As they explored, Elena felt an inexplicable pull towards one particular door at the end of the hall. The wood was dark and weathered, almost as if it were calling to her.

"Here," she said, her heart racing as she reached for the doorknob. It felt cool to the touch, and with a gentle twist, she opened the door.

The sight before them took her breath away. The room was small but exquisitely adorned with antique furniture draped in elegant fabrics, long forgotten but still imbued with a sense of grandeur. Sunlight streamed through the windows, illuminating the dust motes that danced in the air like spirits from the past.

But what caught her eye was a collection of items displayed on a weathered mahogany table at the center of the room. There were delicate letters, their edges frayed and yellowed with age, as well as a series of paintings depicting lovers entwined in passionate embraces, their eyes sparkling with the secrets of their hearts.

"This is incredible," Elena breathed, stepping into the room and feeling an overwhelming sense of connection to the lives that had once filled this space.

"What is this place?" Nathaniel asked, stepping in beside her. "It looks like a shrine to some long-lost romance."

"I think it is," she replied, her fingers brushing over the letters. "These must be the relics of forbidden love. Perhaps these were the letters between Isabella and Edward?"

As she began to sift through the items, she felt a sense of urgency and excitement. One letter in particular caught her eye, sealed with a wax stamp, its inscription elegant and ornate. She carefully opened it, her heart pounding as she began to read:

My Dearest Isabella,

Though the world may conspire to keep us apart, my love for you grows stronger with each passing day. The walls of Hawthorn Hill may hold secrets, but they cannot contain the fire that burns within me for you. Meet me where the willow bends, beneath the stars, where our love can be free.

Yours forever, Edward

Tears pricked at her eyes as she imagined the love that had blossomed in secret, the yearning and desperation that had marked their lives. She felt a rush of empathy for Isabella, whose heart had endured so much pain.

"This is beautiful," Nathaniel said softly, leaning closer to read over her shoulder. "It's like a glimpse into their souls."

"Exactly," Elena replied, her heart swelling with a mix of longing and sorrow. "They were willing to defy the world for love. I wonder what happened to them."

As she delved deeper into the letters, a pattern began to emerge. The correspondence told a tale of passion and longing, of stolen moments and whispered promises. But as she reached the final letter, a chill swept through the room, as if the air itself had thickened with unspoken truths.

Beloved,

I fear for what lies ahead. Forces conspire against us, and I cannot bear the thought of losing you. If fate separates us, know that my love for you will remain, eternal as the stars above. Should you wish to escape this cursed estate, meet me at dawn beneath the willow. We will find our freedom.

Forever yours, Edward

Elena's heart sank as she absorbed the weight of those words. They spoke of a desperate hope that had ultimately been crushed under the weight of societal expectations. She could feel the pain radiating from the pages, the shadows of their love entwined with regret.

"Something terrible happened," she said, her voice trembling. "They were planning to run away, but... but they never made it."

"Isabella's fate was intertwined with this room," Nathaniel murmured, his eyes searching hers. "This is where her heart was broken."

Elena nodded, tears spilling down her cheeks as the tragedy of her ancestors engulfed her. "I need to learn more. There must be more to their story, something that explains why their love was forbidden."

As she looked around the room, she felt the ghosts of her family's past pressing in on her. The air crackled with emotion, and for the first time, she felt a deep connection to the women who had come before her, their struggles echoing through time.

In that moment, Elena understood that her quest was not just about uncovering the truth of Isabella and Edward's love; it was about reclaiming her family's legacy and breaking free from the shadows that had haunted them for generations.

"I won't let their love story end in tragedy," she vowed, looking up at Nathaniel. "Together, we'll find out what happened to them. We'll give them the ending they deserved."

His gaze met hers, filled with fierce determination. "I'm with you, Elena. We'll unravel the secrets of this estate, and in doing so, we'll uncover the truth about our own hearts."

As they stood together amidst the relics of forbidden love, Elena felt the weight of her family's past resting on her shoulders, but she also felt a spark of hope igniting within her. The forbidden room had opened the door to a new chapter—a chapter where they would confront the echoes of loss and seek to honor the love that had endured against all odds.

With Nathaniel by her side, she felt ready to dive into the depths of her ancestors' lives, to unearth the secrets that had been buried in the shadows, and to forge a path toward healing for both their families. Together, they would rewrite the narrative of love lost, transforming it into one of courage, hope, and redemption.

13

The Storm Within Battles of the Heart

Dark clouds gathered ominously above Hawthorn Hill, echoing the turmoil that raged within Elena's heart. The once-sweet scent of autumn leaves now mingled with the sharp tang of impending rain, a prelude to the storm that brewed both outside and within. After uncovering the letters from Isabella and Edward, she had felt an exhilarating connection to the past, yet it also stirred a whirlwind of conflicting emotions that left her reeling.

Elena paced the drawing room, her mind racing. Nathaniel had stepped out to gather more materials from his studio, leaving her alone with her thoughts. She couldn't shake the fear that had settled in her chest like a heavy stone. What if uncovering the past only led to more heartache? The tragic fate of Isabella and Edward loomed like a dark cloud, casting doubt on the potential for her own happiness.

As the wind howled outside, she recalled the urgency in Edward's final letter—the sense of desperation, the plea for freedom. Was it foolish to believe that love could conquer all? Her thoughts flickered to Nathaniel, the way he had looked at her with such intensity, his eyes filled with a mixture of understanding and desire. But could she trust him? Could she trust anyone with her heart after all the pain that had come before?

A sharp clap of thunder jolted her from her reverie, and she moved to the window, watching as the first raindrops began to splatter against the glass. The sky darkened, the landscape transforming into a blurred tableau of gray and green. The storm mirrored her inner turmoil—raging and restless, fueled by fear and longing.

The memory of their recent exploration of the forbidden room played in her mind, and she could almost feel the weight of the past pressing down on her. The relics of love had inspired her to confront her own feelings, but what if her heart was merely echoing the desires of her ancestors?

Could she truly dare to love Nathaniel, or would history repeat itself?

Elena closed her eyes, feeling the vibrations of the thunder rumble through her. She needed to face this storm, to confront her emotions rather than let them overwhelm her. Taking a deep breath, she stepped away from the window and sank into the plush armchair, determined to sort through the chaos of her thoughts.

What do you want, Elena? The question echoed in her mind, a whisper of clarity amid the tumult.

With her eyes closed, she envisioned Nathaniel—his brooding expression, the way his lips curved into a smile when he was passionate about his art, the warmth of his presence. *He makes me feel alive.*

Yet, the fear was palpable. Could she allow herself to feel that spark when the shadows of tragedy loomed so close? The specter of Isabella's heartbreak haunted her thoughts. She could hear her great-grandmother's silent cry echoing through the halls of Hawthorn Hill, warning her against the dangers of love.

Just then, the door creaked open, and Nathaniel stepped in, shaking raindrops from his hair. The sight of him sent a jolt through her, an electrifying mix of desire and apprehension. He met her gaze, his brow furrowed with concern.

"Elena, are you all right?" he asked, stepping closer. "You look troubled."

She hesitated, the words tumbling in her throat, caught between the urge to share her fears and the instinct to shield her heart. "I just... I've been thinking about everything we've uncovered. The letters, the forbidden love... it's all so overwhelming."

He took a seat across from her, his expression softening. "It is a lot to process. But we can face it together."

"Can we really?" she whispered, the weight of uncertainty pressing down on her. "What if we're just repeating the mistakes of the past? What if my heart leads me to the same fate as Isabella's?"

Nathaniel's expression shifted, a flicker of understanding crossing his face. "Elena, I can't promise that we'll have a perfect ending. But I can promise that I will always be honest with you, and I'll fight for us."

Tears prickled at the corners of her eyes, the mixture of fear and hope threatening to overwhelm her. "But what if it's not enough? What if I lose everything?"

He leaned forward, his voice steady and filled with warmth. "Then we'll build something new together. We're not our ancestors. We have the chance to rewrite our story."

As his words sank in, a flicker of hope ignited within her, battling against the shadows of doubt. She realized how deeply she craved that connection—the authenticity of sharing her heart with someone who understood her fears and desires.

The wind outside howled, rattling the windows, but in that moment, Elena felt a surge of defiance rising within her. She was not going to let the storms—both within and outside—define her fate. It was time to embrace the possibility of love, to trust her heart even amidst the chaos.

Taking a deep breath, she met Nathaniel's gaze, a sense of determination washing over her. "You're right. We're not Isabella and Edward. We have the power to choose our own path, to create our own love story."

Nathaniel's eyes sparkled with encouragement, and she could see the flicker of hope mirrored in his gaze. "Exactly. Together, we can weather any storm."

And in that moment, amidst the growing storm, Elena took a leap of faith. She reached for Nathaniel's hand, intertwining her fingers with his, feeling the warmth of his skin against hers. "I want to trust you, Nathaniel. I want to embrace this. My feelings for you… they're real."

A smile broke across his face, illuminating the shadows that had lingered in the corners of the room. "Then let's face whatever comes our way, together."

As they sat there, hands clasped, the storm outside intensified, but inside the drawing room, a different kind of tempest began to shift.

The fear that had gripped Elena's heart loosened its hold, giving way to a burgeoning sense of hope.

The winds outside may rage and howl, but within her, a quiet strength began to grow—a resolve to trust in love and to fight for the future she longed for. Together, they would navigate the storm, not just for themselves but for the echoes of those who had come before.

As the thunder rumbled overhead, Elena found solace in Nathaniel's presence, feeling a profound connection between them. In this moment, she chose to embrace the uncertainty, to step into the unknown with courage and heart.

And so, as the storm swirled around Hawthorn Hill, the battle within Elena transformed into a steadfast determination to love fiercely, to trust deeply, and to honor the legacy of love that had withstood the test of time.

14

Love in the Shadows
A Growing Darkness

The days following their emotional revelation were a whirlwind of passion and tenderness. Elena and Nathaniel spent every moment they could together, wandering the estate's vast grounds, exploring the wild beauty of Yorkshire that surrounded Hawthorn Hill. The autumn leaves painted the landscape in shades of gold and crimson, mirroring the warmth blooming in her heart.

Yet, beneath the surface of their burgeoning romance, dark clouds loomed—threatening storms of jealousy and family obligations that neither of them could ignore.

As they strolled through the gardens, Nathaniel would occasionally pause to sketch the vibrant foliage, his concentration intense, and Elena would watch him with admiration. There was a magic in the way he translated the world around him onto paper, capturing fleeting moments with strokes of charcoal. However, each time she saw him immersed in his art, a flicker of unease ignited within her. She couldn't shake the feeling that others were watching them, their budding love a potential scandal in the eyes of the townsfolk and the very walls of her own family estate.

One evening, as the sun dipped below the horizon, casting long shadows across the garden, Elena found herself standing at the edge of the estate's formal garden. The air was crisp, and the scent of damp earth filled her lungs. Lost in thought, she replayed conversations with her mother in her mind, the disapproval she'd sensed whenever Nathaniel's name was mentioned.

"Elena! You must think of your future!" her mother had scolded just days ago, her voice a stern reminder of the responsibilities that came with their family's legacy. "You can't throw your heart away on some brooding artist. You must consider the Hawthorne name!"

But how could she dismiss the connection she felt with Nathaniel? The laughter they shared, the comfort of their conversations, the way he looked at her as if she were the only light in his world—it was all too precious to let slip away.

"Penny for your thoughts?" Nathaniel's voice pulled her from her reverie, and she turned to find him standing behind her, a teasing smile on his lips and charcoal smudged on his fingers.

Elena smiled back, but the weight of her thoughts still hung heavy. "Just... thinking about how quickly things are changing."

"Good changes, I hope." He stepped closer, brushing his fingertips against her cheek, sending warmth through her.

"Yes, but... what about the future?" she replied, her voice barely a whisper. "What will happen when my family finds out about us?"

His expression shifted, the playful glimmer in his eyes replaced with a serious intensity. "We'll face it together, Elena. I won't let anything come between us."

Before she could respond, a sudden rustle nearby made them both turn. A group of townsfolk had entered the garden, their voices carrying through the crisp evening air. Elena's heart sank as she recognized them—friends of her mother, all of whom would surely gossip about her relationship with Nathaniel, the enigmatic artist from the village.

"Look at that!" one of them exclaimed, her voice dripping with mockery. "The Hawthorne heiress, gallivanting with a common painter. What would the family say?"

Elena felt the heat rise in her cheeks as the group laughed, their voices echoing like a taunt through the garden. Nathaniel stiffened beside her, his jaw tightening as he glanced at the intruders.

"Don't listen to them," he murmured, his voice low. "They don't know what we have."

But the shadows of their words clung to Elena like a shroud. "It's not just them, Nathaniel. My family has expectations—traditions they want me to uphold. They won't accept this."

"Then we'll make them understand," he replied, determination edging his tone. "We can't let anyone dictate how we feel."

Elena wanted to believe him, to trust in the strength of their love. But just then, a familiar figure appeared at the garden's entrance— her mother, Lady Hawthorne, stepping into view with an expression of disapproval etched across her features. The townsfolk fell silent, their laughter fading as they realized the gravity of the moment.

"Elena," her mother called, her voice sharp enough to cut through the tension. "What on earth are you doing out here?"

Elena's heart raced as she exchanged a glance with Nathaniel, who stepped slightly closer, as if to shield her from her mother's judgment. "I was just enjoying the garden," she replied, trying to sound casual, though the weight of her mother's gaze felt suffocating.

Her mother's eyes flicked over Nathaniel, a disapproving arch of her brow signaling her discontent. "With him?" she asked, her voice dripping with disdain. "You know it is not proper for you to be seen with someone of his... standing."

"I care about him, Mother," Elena replied, her voice steadier than she felt. "You don't understand—"

"Understand what?" Lady Hawthorne interjected, her tone icy. "That you're throwing away your future for a whim? I won't allow it. The Hawthorne name is built on tradition, on duty. You have responsibilities, Elena!"

"I want to make my own choices!" Elena shot back, a fire igniting within her. "This is my life, not just a legacy to uphold. Can't you see that?"

Nathaniel remained silent at her side, his presence a steady comfort, yet she could feel the tension radiating from him. Lady Hawthorne's glare shifted to him, as if sensing the source of her daughter's rebellion.

"This is not a conversation to have in front of him," her mother said, her voice low and controlled, laced with authority. "You will come inside at once."

Elena's heart sank at the command, feeling torn between her mother's expectations and her fierce desire for love and independence. But as she looked at Nathaniel, the resolve in his eyes gave her the strength to fight.

"I won't let you dictate my heart," she declared, the words spilling out before she could think better of them. "I deserve the chance to explore this. To explore us."

A sharp silence followed, and her mother's eyes flared with a mix of anger and disbelief. "You're being foolish, Elena. This will ruin you."

"No, Mother," she countered, her voice stronger than she expected. "You don't get to decide what my happiness looks like. I'm not a pawn in your game."

In that moment, Elena felt a wave of freedom wash over her, mingled with the fear of the consequences to come. But as she glanced back at Nathaniel, she saw admiration in his gaze—a silent promise of solidarity that bolstered her resolve.

Lady Hawthorne's expression hardened, the lines of worry etching deeper into her brow. "You have no idea the weight of what you're defying. You'll regret this."

With that, she turned on her heel and strode away, her presence a storm cloud hanging over them. The townsfolk whispered among themselves, their eyes wide with shock and intrigue, leaving Elena feeling exposed and raw.

"I'm so sorry," she breathed, turning to Nathaniel, her heart racing. "I didn't mean to—"

"Don't apologize," he interrupted, his expression fierce and passionate. "You stood up for what you believe in. That's brave, Elena."

"But it might cost us everything," she said, a tremor of fear creeping into her voice.

"No." He took her hands in his, grounding her. "It's the first step towards carving our own path. We can't let their shadows consume us. We have to fight for this—fight for us."

But as they stood together in the fading light, Elena couldn't shake the feeling of uncertainty settling deep within her. With each passing day, it became clearer that their love would not come without sacrifice. The storm of jealousy and obligation loomed large, and though her heart yearned for Nathaniel, she felt the shadows growing ever closer.

As night fell, the wind picked up, rustling through the trees, echoing the tumult in her soul. Elena knew that the road ahead would be fraught with challenges, but she was determined to face them head-on. For in the depths of her heart, she believed that love could triumph even in the darkest of shadows.

Together, they would navigate the storms, but as the first hints of a growing darkness settled in the corners of her mind, she couldn't help but wonder if their love was strong enough to withstand the trials that lay ahead.

15

The Winter's Embrace Frozen in Time

As winter blanketed Hawthorn Hill in a thick layer of snow, the estate transformed into a breathtaking spectacle of white—a frozen wonderland that glimmered beneath the pale sun. Each branch was coated with frost, each pathway lined with shimmering crystals, and the world outside felt suspended in time. But inside the grand estate, the atmosphere was anything but serene.

Elena peered out the window of her room, watching as the snowflakes swirled in a mesmerizing dance. It was beautiful, but it also felt like a barrier—a wall that separated her from the world she longed to embrace. Despite the idyllic scenery, a chill had settled deep within her heart, mirroring the frost creeping into every corner of the estate.

Since that fateful evening when she had stood her ground against her mother, the tension between Elena and Nathaniel had only deepened. Their stolen moments in the garden had turned into hesitant exchanges, the passion that had once ignited their connection now tempered by uncertainty and unspoken fears.

She felt the weight of her family's expectations pressing down on her, stifling the warmth of her feelings for Nathaniel. Her mother's warnings echoed in her mind, freezing her heart with doubt. Could she truly defy tradition for the sake of love? Would it be enough to bridge the widening chasm between them?

"Are you ready for our walk?" Nathaniel's voice pulled her from her thoughts. He stood at her door, bundled in a thick coat, his cheeks flushed from the cold. The sight of him ignited a flicker of warmth in her chest, but the chill of their recent distance loomed large.

"I... I don't know," she replied, hesitating as she smoothed her skirts, a nervous habit that had surfaced since their argument. "It's so cold outside. Are you sure you want to?"

His brows furrowed slightly, and she could see the flicker of frustration in his eyes. "We can't let the cold keep us inside forever. We need to talk about what's happening between us, Elena."

She bit her lip, the conflict roiling within her. "I know, but I—"

"Then let's take a walk," he insisted gently, stepping closer. "It's the only way we can clear the air."

With a reluctant sigh, Elena relented and nodded. "Okay, let's go."

Bundling herself in her own coat, she followed Nathaniel out of the estate, the cold air hitting her face like a sharp slap. The beauty of the snow-covered landscape was breathtaking, but the weight of their unresolved emotions hung heavily in the air.

As they walked along the path that wound through the estate's gardens, the world around them was eerily silent, the only sound being the crunch of snow beneath their boots. It was beautiful yet haunting, much like their relationship at that moment.

"I miss the way we used to be," Nathaniel finally said, breaking the silence, his voice heavy with unspoken emotions. "We were so connected, and now…" He trailed off, running a gloved hand through his hair in frustration.

"I do too," Elena admitted, feeling a pang of longing in her heart. "But everything feels so complicated now. I can't shake the feeling that my family will never accept you."

"Maybe they don't have to accept me," he replied, his tone laced with determination. "What matters is how you feel. We can create our own family, our own traditions. We don't have to live by anyone else's rules."

The passion in his voice sparked something inside her—a flicker of hope against the encroaching chill. "I want to believe that," she said softly, stopping to look into his eyes. "But it's so hard. I feel like I'm stuck between two worlds, and I don't know how to choose."

Nathaniel stepped closer, the warmth of his body radiating against the winter's bite. "Elena, don't you see? Choosing you is the most important thing. We can't let fear dictate our lives. Love is worth the fight."

But even as he spoke those words, Elena felt a tremor of doubt creeping in. *Was love truly enough to overcome the obstacles they faced?* The frozen landscape seemed to echo her turmoil, a reflection of her inner struggle.

"Maybe you're right," she finally said, her voice a whisper. "But what if I lose everything? What if my mother cuts me off, or I disappoint my family? I can't bear the thought of losing you or them."

Nathaniel's expression softened, and he reached out to tuck a loose strand of hair behind her ear, his touch lingering for a moment longer than necessary. "Then let's not focus on what we might lose. Let's focus on what we can build together."

Elena's heart raced at the intensity of his gaze, the way he made her feel as though she were the only person in the world. But even as desire flared within her, a sense of dread washed over her.

"Building something new feels like a risk I'm not ready to take," she admitted, the truth weighing heavily on her tongue. "The stakes feel too high."

He took a step back, the warmth between them feeling like a distant memory. "I understand. But just remember, every choice comes with a risk, Elena. What matters is whether the reward is worth it."

The air crackled with tension as they stood facing each other, the cold creeping into their shared silence. Elena's heart felt heavy as she struggled to articulate the thoughts swirling in her mind. "What if we're meant to be, but the world keeps us apart?"

Nathaniel's eyes darkened with determination. "Then we'll find a way to break those barriers. I refuse to let your family's expectations dictate our lives. Love shouldn't come with conditions."

She wanted to reach for him, to close the distance and surrender to the warmth of their connection. But doubt held her back like ice, a numbing reminder of the weight of tradition and family expectations.

The snow continued to fall gently around them, swirling like the thoughts in her head. She took a deep breath, steeling herself against the surge of emotion. "But I can't just turn my back on my family. I owe them so much."

"Then let's prove to them that love is worth fighting for," Nathaniel urged, his voice growing more impassioned. "If we can show them the strength of what we have, maybe they'll understand."

Elena's heart raced at the thought, hope warring with fear. *Could they truly bridge the gap between their worlds?*

"Promise me," she said, her voice trembling, "that you won't give up on us, no matter how hard it gets."

"I promise," he said, his gaze steady and unwavering. "I'll fight for you, for us. I won't let fear stand in the way of our love."

As they stood there, the chill of winter enveloping them, a flicker of warmth ignited within her heart. Though the road ahead was fraught with challenges, Elena felt a glimmer of hope take root. Perhaps they could carve a path through the frozen landscape of their lives, transforming it into something beautiful and new.

With renewed determination, she stepped forward, closing the distance between them. "Then let's face it together. Whatever comes our way, we'll figure it out."

Nathaniel's expression brightened, relief flooding his features as he took her hands in his, warmth radiating from his touch. "Together," he echoed, the promise hanging in the air between them like a vow.

As they stood entwined in each other's arms, the winter landscape surrounding them felt a little less cold, a little less daunting. In that moment, they chose love—a choice that would define their path amid the frost and shadows.

And as they turned to walk back toward the estate, hearts intertwined against the encroaching chill, Elena knew that winter would not last forever. With each step, they forged a path toward spring—a season of renewal, of hope, and of love that would endure even the harshest storms.

16

Beneath the Surface Hidden Currents

The winter winds howled outside, a reminder of the world's harshness beyond the comforting walls of Hawthorn Hill. As snow continued to blanket the grounds, Elena found herself drawn deeper into the estate's archives, determined to uncover the secrets of her family's lineage. The old manor seemed to hold its breath as if anticipating her discoveries, its creaking floorboards whispering long-forgotten tales of love, loss, and sacrifice.

Elena had spent the last few days in the dusty library, combing through her ancestors' letters and journals. Each page felt like a window into the past, revealing fragments of lives once lived, joys and heartaches woven into the fabric of her family's history. The scent of aged paper and ink filled the air, a comforting aroma that wrapped around her like a warm blanket.

She paused over a particularly worn journal, its leather cover cracked and faded. Opening it, she was immediately drawn into the vivid emotions of her great-grandmother, Eliza Hawthorne. Eliza's words danced across the pages, filled with longing and desperation, as she wrote about a forbidden romance that echoed with a haunting familiarity.

"I knew he was the one," Eliza wrote in one entry, her script sharp with emotion. "But our families would never allow it. He is a mere artist, an outsider, and I am bound to this estate, to my family's name. What choice do I have but to suppress my heart?"

As Elena read, a chill crept up her spine. She recognized the same tumultuous emotions swirling within her own heart, the echoes of Eliza's struggles mirroring her own. It was as if she were peering into a mirror reflecting her deepest desires and fears.

Turning another page, she stumbled upon a sketch that had been tucked between the leaves. It was a portrait of a man, his features strikingly handsome, his eyes filled with a tempest of emotion that seemed to leap from the paper. A name was scrawled beneath the sketch: *Thomas Blackwood*.

"Who are you?" Elena whispered to the shadows of the past. The name was unfamiliar, but the intensity of his gaze sent a shiver through her. She felt a strange connection, as if he were calling out to her from the depths of history.

Determined to learn more, Elena sought out the estate's records, hoping to uncover the story of Thomas Blackwood. As she delved deeper, she found more mentions of him—letters exchanged between him and Eliza, tales of their clandestine meetings beneath the ancient oak tree that still stood in the garden.

The letters spoke of stolen moments, of whispers shared beneath the stars, and of the heartache that ensued when Eliza's family found out about their affair. It was a tragic tale of love thwarted by societal expectations, a love that had ignited a fire within her great-grandmother's heart, only to be extinguished by duty and tradition.

Elena felt a pang of sympathy for Eliza, but she also felt something else—an awakening of her own hidden desires. As she immersed herself in the story, she began to question her own feelings for Nathaniel. Was she allowing fear to dictate her heart? Was her family's legacy worth sacrificing her happiness?

That evening, as the sun dipped below the horizon and the shadows of dusk enveloped the estate, Elena decided to confront her own emotions. She wandered to the oak tree, the very place where her great-grandmother had once dreamed of a life filled with love, free from the burdens of her lineage. The tree, now heavy with snow, stood like a sentinel, a witness to the passage of time and the love stories that had unfolded beneath its boughs.

Nathaniel arrived shortly after, his breath visible in the cold air, his eyes brightening at the sight of her. "I thought I might find you here," he said, stepping closer, a smile tugging at the corners of his lips. "You've been lost in those books again, haven't you?"

She nodded, her heart racing at the prospect of sharing her discoveries with him. "There's so much I didn't know about my family. They had their own struggles, their own loves that were forbidden. It's… it's opened my eyes."

"What have you found?" he asked, his interest piqued as he moved to stand beside her, both of them looking up at the ancient tree.

Elena took a deep breath, the weight of her thoughts swirling inside her. "My great-grandmother, Eliza, fell in love with a man named Thomas Blackwood. Their love was fierce, but it was deemed unacceptable. They were forced apart by their families, and it broke her heart."

Nathaniel's expression softened as he listened, the intensity of his gaze making her heart flutter. "That sounds tragic," he murmured. "But it also shows the strength of love."

"Yes," she agreed, her voice trembling. "But it also makes me question everything. Eliza's story is a warning, isn't it? She lost everything because she defied her family. What if I do the same?"

Nathaniel took her hands, his warmth a stark contrast to the chill surrounding them. "Elena, love is worth the risk. You've seen how deeply your great-grandmother felt, how powerful her emotions were. Don't you want to experience that kind of love? To follow your heart?"

"But what if it ends in tragedy, like it did for Eliza?" she challenged, her voice laced with uncertainty.

"Then at least you will have lived fully," he replied, his voice steady and sincere. "You can't live in fear of the past. It's time to carve your own path, to embrace your desires without letting history dictate your choices."

His words resonated deep within her, igniting a flame of courage she hadn't known she possessed. As she gazed into his eyes, she felt the barriers she had erected begin to crumble. "I don't want to be like Eliza," she confessed. "But I can't help but feel connected to her, to her pain and her dreams."

"Then let that connection guide you, not bind you," Nathaniel urged, stepping closer, their bodies inches apart. "You can honor her memory by choosing a different path—a path that leads to love, not despair."

The sincerity in his voice warmed her heart, and she felt a wave of determination wash over her. "You're right," she said softly, her voice barely above a whisper. "I can't allow fear to control me. I want to embrace what we have, no matter the consequences."

Nathaniel's eyes sparkled with hope, and he took a step closer, wrapping his arms around her waist, drawing her in. "Then let's create our own story, one that defies the past and embraces the future."

Elena's heart raced as she felt the heat of his body against hers, a warmth that melted away the chill of winter and the doubts that had haunted her. "I want that," she breathed, leaning into him, the world around them fading into the background.

As they stood beneath the ancient oak tree, the wind swirling around them like a gentle caress, Elena felt the weight of her lineage shift. She was no longer merely a reflection of her family's past; she was forging her own path, ready to embrace the love that had blossomed in the shadows.

Together, they would navigate the hidden currents of their hearts, challenging the ghosts of the past while forging a new legacy—one filled with passion, courage, and an unwavering belief that love could conquer all.

In that moment, as their lips brushed against each other, the snow began to fall again, blanketing the ground with new beginnings. Beneath the surface of their fears and doubts, the currents of love surged forward, ready to carry them into a future bright with promise and hope.

101 Storms of Hawthorn Hill

17

The Rebellion Love's Defiance

The dawn of a new day brought with it an invigorating chill, a crisp reminder that winter still held sway over Hawthorn Hill. But within Elena, a warmth blossomed—a determination that ignited her spirit like the first light of spring breaking through the frost. She had made her choice; the moment had arrived to defy the shackles of her family's expectations and embrace the love that had ignited her heart.

As she dressed that morning, her fingers brushed against the fabric of her gown, a vibrant emerald green that mirrored the lush spring foliage she longed to see. The color felt like a rebellion against the muted tones of her family's traditions. She caught her reflection in the mirror, the woman staring back at her was not just the dutiful daughter of the Hawthorne lineage; she was Elena—a woman ready to seize her own fate.

Stepping into the breakfast room, she found her mother seated at the table, the morning light illuminating the lines of worry etched on her face. The air was thick with unspoken tension, the shadows of their recent arguments lingering like a storm cloud waiting to unleash its fury.

"Good morning, Mother," Elena said, forcing herself to sound cheerful, despite the weight of her resolve pressing down on her.

"Good morning, Elena." Her mother looked up, her expression unreadable. "I trust you're well? I hope you've been keeping busy with your studies."

"Yes, quite busy," Elena replied, her heart pounding as she considered her next words. "But I've also spent time with Nathaniel. He's been very helpful with my research on our family history."

Her mother's brow furrowed, an unmistakable flicker of disapproval passing across her features. "You know how I feel about that boy. He is not suitable for you, Elena. You must think of your future."

"I can't do that anymore," Elena declared, her voice steady despite the tumult within. "I can't continue to hide from my own desires. I love Nathaniel, and I intend to be with him."

The words hung in the air like thunder, crackling with a fierce energy that both frightened and exhilarated her. Her mother's eyes widened in disbelief, shock etching itself into her features. "You *what?*"

"I love him," Elena repeated, her heart racing as she stood her ground. "He makes me feel alive, and I refuse to let my family's expectations dictate my happiness."

"Do you hear yourself?" her mother replied, her voice rising. "You would throw away everything—your reputation, your future—over a mere infatuation?"

"It's not an infatuation, Mother! It's real," Elena insisted, her heart pounding. "And if you can't accept that, then I will have to make my own choices. I cannot live in a gilded cage any longer."

With that, Elena turned on her heel and stormed out of the room, the clatter of her heart echoing in her ears. She hurried up the staircase, the floorboards creaking beneath her feet, each step feeling like a declaration of her newfound freedom.

As she reached her room, she closed the door behind her and leaned against it, allowing herself a moment to breathe. The exhilaration of her defiance surged through her veins, drowning out the fear that had once held her captive.

Today was a turning point. No longer would she be the obedient daughter trapped in the expectations of her family; she would be the woman who pursued love and happiness on her own terms.

Her thoughts turned to Nathaniel, the spark of passion igniting once more. She couldn't wait to share her decision with him, to unveil her heart and let the flames of their love consume the doubts and fears that had plagued them.

Leaving her room, she rushed down the winding staircase and out into the snow-laden gardens. The cold air was invigorating, filling her lungs with life as she strode towards the oak tree where they had shared their first kiss.

Nathaniel was already there, standing beneath the old oak, his breath clouding in the frigid air. He looked up, his expression shifting from surprise to joy as he spotted her. "Elena! I was just thinking about you."

"I have something to tell you," she said, her heart racing with anticipation. "I've decided to defy my family. I won't let their expectations control my life any longer. I want to be with you, Nathaniel."

His eyes widened in disbelief, then filled with warmth and admiration. "Are you serious?" he asked, stepping closer, his voice low and intense. "You're willing to risk everything for us?"

"Yes," she replied, feeling the weight of her decision settle into place. "I realize now that I can't live for anyone else's dreams but my own. You make me feel alive, and I won't give that up."

A radiant smile broke across Nathaniel's face, transforming his features. "Elena, you have no idea how much this means to me. I've been so afraid that you would choose duty over love."

"I won't do that," she said, her heart soaring as she reached for his hand, intertwining their fingers. "Love is worth fighting for. I refuse to let fear dictate my choices any longer."

They stood together beneath the ancient oak, the wind rustling the branches overhead, as if nature itself was celebrating their rebellion. The snowflakes danced around them, a whirlwind of white that felt like the promise of new beginnings.

"Let's not waste any more time," Nathaniel said, his gaze burning with intensity. "Let's make our love known. We can defy the odds together."

Elena felt a thrill at the prospect, her heart racing with excitement and trepidation. "Yes, let's do it. But how?"

"We could start by simply being ourselves, openly," he suggested, his voice low and earnest. "We could attend the village dance next week. If we stand together, they'll have no choice but to see our love."

The idea sent a rush of exhilaration coursing through her veins. "Yes! I want to show the world that we belong together."

As they spoke, the sun began to break through the clouds, casting a warm glow over the landscape. It felt as though the world was shifting to accommodate their resolve, as if nature itself was celebrating their love.

Their lips met in a fierce kiss, the taste of snow mingling with the warmth of their passion. It was a kiss that sealed their defiance, a promise to stand united against whatever challenges lay ahead.

As they pulled away, breathless and exhilarated, Elena realized that this was more than just a declaration of love; it was a rebellion against the constraints that had bound her. Together, they would carve out their own destiny, undeterred by the whispers of the past.

"I feel like I can take on the world," she said, her eyes sparkling with determination.

"And you can," Nathaniel replied, his voice filled with conviction. "As long as we stand together, there's nothing we can't face."

With renewed energy, they began to walk hand in hand through the gardens, the world around them sparkling with possibility. The oak tree stood as a witness to their newfound commitment, the weight of their love breaking the chains of tradition and expectation.

Elena knew that the path ahead wouldn't be easy; there would be storms to weather and obstacles to overcome. But for the first time, she felt truly free—free to love, to dream, and to live for herself. In Nathaniel, she had found a partner who understood the depths of her soul, and together they would forge a future that was uniquely theirs.

As they ventured deeper into the gardens, laughter and love intertwined, their hearts beating in unison, Elena realized that rebellion was not just an act of defiance; it was an embrace of everything she had ever wanted. With every step they took, they were writing their own story—one filled with love's fierce defiance, ready to alter their destinies forever.

18

The Cursed History Legacies of the Past

The vibrant energy of Elena's newfound love with Nathaniel felt electric, igniting a fire within her that she had long thought extinguished. But as the snow began to melt and spring cautiously approached Hawthorn Hill, she knew she could not ignore the whispers of the past that haunted the estate. Curiosity and trepidation intertwined within her, compelling her to delve deeper into the mysteries that had once captivated her interest.

With determination, Elena set aside her studies and returned to the dusty archives in the estate's library. She felt as though she were stepping into a time capsule, each book and letter filled with remnants of a lineage laden with secrets. Her fingers brushed against the spines of worn volumes, each holding the promise of new discoveries.

It was a collection of old town records that first drew her attention, dusty tomes bound in cracked leather. She pulled one from the shelf and opened it, the pages yellowed with age, revealing a list of families in the Yorkshire area and their respective histories. As she leafed through the fragile pages, her heart raced at the possibility of uncovering more about her own lineage.

But it was not long before her eyes landed on a familiar name—Hawthorne. The name leapt out at her, drawing her closer as she read about the estate's early days. The words were laced with an unsettling tone, hinting at a darkness that had seeped into the very foundation of her ancestral home.

"...the Hawthornes were cursed, a bloodline tainted by betrayal and sorrow. Generations have been lost to the shadows of their own making, each plagued by the tragic fate of their forebears."

Elena's breath caught in her throat as she read on, the words wrapping around her like a shroud. According to the record, the curse had originated from a scandalous affair centuries ago—a love that had defied the laws of nature and society, leading to betrayal, jealousy, and a terrible retribution from the spirit world.

"Legend has it that the original owner of Hawthorn Hill, Edmund Hawthorne, fell in love with a woman forbidden to him by family ties. In a fit of rage, her brother confronted Edmund, leading to a tragic duel. The brother was slain, and as he drew his last breath, he cursed the Hawthorne name, vowing that no descendant would find lasting happiness."

Elena's heart sank. The weight of the curse felt palpable, pressing against her chest. Each generation, it seemed, had faced its own heartache, with marriages falling apart, loves lost, and tragedies shadowing their lives.

"What have you done to me?" she murmured, the chill of realization creeping into her bones. Could the curse truly have any bearing on her love for Nathaniel? Could it threaten their budding romance?

The thought sent a shiver down her spine. Desperate for clarity, she turned to the next volume, flipping through the pages until she came across accounts of her family members, their fates meticulously documented. Her great-grandmother, Eliza, had been a victim of the curse; her love for Thomas Blackwood had ended in heartbreak, much like the generations before her.

Elena's mind whirled with the implications. Would her love for Nathaniel, too, be destined for tragedy? Would she be the next in line to face the consequences of her ancestors' mistakes? The prospect filled her with dread, but she knew she could not let fear control her. Instead, she had to confront this legacy head-on.

With a deep breath, she gathered her courage and decided to speak with Nathaniel. She needed him to understand the history that loomed over them like a dark cloud, threatening to drown out the light they had found together.

Later that afternoon, she found Nathaniel in the small art studio he had set up in the village, surrounded by canvases splashed with color that contrasted sharply with the oppressive atmosphere she had been grappling with. His brow furrowed in concentration as he painted, the soft light of the studio casting a warm glow around him.

"Nathaniel?" she called softly, stepping into the room. He looked up, his expression brightening at the sight of her.

"Elena! You're here!" He set aside his brush and wiped his hands on a rag, stepping closer to embrace her. The warmth of his body was a balm to her troubled heart.

"I need to talk to you about something important," she said, the weight of her news pressing down on her.

His expression shifted, concern etching itself into his features. "What's wrong? You look troubled."

Elena hesitated, but she knew there was no turning back. "I've been researching our family's history, and I found something alarming—a curse that has plagued the Hawthorne lineage for generations."

Nathaniel's brow furrowed in confusion. "A curse? What do you mean?"

She took a deep breath and recounted the tale she had read about Edmund Hawthorne and the tragic history that had unfolded at Hawthorn Hill. As she spoke, she could see his expression shift from confusion to concern, the weight of her words sinking in.

"So you're saying that our love could be cursed?" he asked, his voice low.

"Yes," she replied, her heart heavy. "It seems that every generation has faced heartbreak, loss, and tragedy. I can't help but wonder if we are doomed to follow the same path."

Nathaniel stepped back, a mix of frustration and disbelief clouding his eyes. "You can't believe in that! It's just a story—a myth designed to scare us. We can't let tales of the past dictate our future."

Elena felt a flicker of anger rise within her. "But what if there's truth to it? My great-grandmother's love ended in heartache, just like all the others. I don't want to lose you, Nathaniel. I can't bear the thought of repeating their mistakes."

Nathaniel closed the distance between them, taking her hands in his. "Elena, we are not our ancestors. We have the power to change our fate. We can break this cycle; we can forge our own path."

"But how?" she asked, her voice trembling. "What if the curse is real?"

"Then we fight against it together," he replied, his eyes fierce with determination. "We face whatever comes our way, side by side. Love isn't meant to be easy; it's about perseverance, about standing strong against the storms."

His words resonated within her, igniting a spark of hope. Perhaps they could defy the curse. Perhaps they could choose a different path — one where love triumphed over the darkness that had haunted her family for centuries.

"But what if it destroys us?" she whispered, the fear still lingering in her heart.

Nathaniel brushed a strand of hair behind her ear, his touch gentle yet firm. "Then we go down fighting. But I refuse to let fear dictate our love. We have a chance to rewrite the narrative, to carve out a future that belongs to us. But we must face it together."

Elena searched his eyes, seeking the truth in his words. As she gazed into his warm, unwavering gaze, she felt her resolve strengthen. Together, they could confront the legacy that threatened to tear them apart. They could shatter the bonds of the past and create their own destiny.

"Okay," she said softly, determination rising within her. "Let's confront this together. Let's discover the truth behind the curse and find a way to break it."

A smile broke across Nathaniel's face, his relief palpable. "That's the spirit. We will not let this curse define us. We'll delve into the history and find a way to free your family from its grip."

As they stood together in the studio, the warmth of their connection radiated like a beacon, cutting through the shadows that threatened to consume them. In that moment, Elena understood that their love was more powerful than any curse. Together, they would explore the depths of their family history, unearthing the truth behind the darkness that had plagued the Hawthorne name.

With newfound determination, they left the studio hand in hand, ready to face whatever challenges lay ahead. They would confront the cursed history together, forging a bond that would withstand the test of time and defy the legacy that had sought to destroy them.

As they stepped into the crisp spring air, Elena felt a sense of hope blooming within her—a promise that, no matter the obstacles they faced, love would guide them through the shadows and into the light.

19

Heartbreak and Healing
The Calm After the Storm

The world outside Hawthorn Hill had transformed after the storm, its fierce winds now replaced by a haunting stillness. The air felt heavy with unspoken words, the landscape bathed in a soft, muted light that mirrored Elena's turbulent heart. The storm had passed, but its aftermath left a gaping chasm in her soul, a wound too fresh to touch.

In the days following the devastating revelation about Nathaniel's connection to her family's curse, Elena withdrew into herself. The vibrant colors of spring that had begun to bloom around the estate seemed to pale in comparison to the dull ache that consumed her. Each day felt like a battle against the rising tide of sadness that threatened to drown her.

Elena spent long hours in her room, staring out of the window at the gardens that were once her refuge. The flowers swayed gently in the breeze, their bright petals reaching for the sun, while she remained rooted in the shadows. Memories of laughter and shared dreams with Nathaniel played like a haunting melody in her mind, each note tinged with sorrow.

In her solitude, Elena replayed the moment when Nathaniel had confessed his lineage—a revelation that had shattered her heart. He had discovered that his great-grandfather was the brother of the man who had been killed by her ancestor, the very cause of the curse that haunted the Hawthorne name. The realization felt like a cruel twist of fate, an invisible thread binding them together in a tragedy they had never chosen.

"What do we do now?" she had asked, her voice trembling as the weight of their history bore down on her.

Nathaniel's expression had darkened, a mix of anger and despair flashing across his face. "It's not your fault, Elena! But I can't help feeling that this will tear us apart."

In that moment, the invisible barrier had risen between them—a wall built on shared sorrow and guilt. Despite the love that still flickered between them, it felt insurmountable. After that day, the conversations that once flowed effortlessly turned into awkward silences, the warmth of their connection replaced by an icy distance. Each time she glanced his way, a pang of longing pierced her heart, reminding her of what they had lost.

As the days passed, Elena found herself wandering the halls of Hawthorn Hill aimlessly, searching for solace in the remnants of her family's history. She explored the dusty corners of the estate, hoping to unearth some forgotten relic that could provide clarity or understanding. Instead, she found only echoes of a past that weighed heavily on her spirit.

One evening, she ventured into the old drawing room, where the faded portraits of her ancestors lined the walls, their expressions both regal and melancholic. As she studied their faces, she felt an overwhelming sense of connection, a shared burden of heartbreak that transcended time.

"Why must love be so complicated?" she whispered to the empty room, her voice barely audible against the silence. "Why must our happiness be marred by the sins of those who came before us?"

Her gaze settled on a portrait of Eliza Hawthorne, her great-grandmother, whose beauty had captivated many, yet whose eyes betrayed a deep sadness. Elena could see the parallels—the longing for love, the struggle against familial expectations, the shadow of a curse lurking just beyond the veil of happiness.

In that moment, Elena realized she was not alone in her pain. Her ancestors had faced their own heartbreaks and had navigated the treacherous waters of love and loss. She could almost hear their voices whispering through the generations, urging her to find strength amidst the despair.

Days turned into weeks, and although the pain of her separation from Nathaniel was sharp, a sense of determination began to blossom within her. She couldn't change the past, but she could choose how to face the future. The more she learned about her family's history, the more she felt a sense of responsibility—not just for her own happiness, but for the healing of the wounds that had marred her lineage.

With renewed resolve, Elena decided to confront Nathaniel, to seek understanding rather than avoidance. She could not allow the curse to dictate her life any longer, and she would not allow fear to overshadow their love.

As she prepared to leave her room, she caught a glimpse of herself in the mirror—her eyes were puffy from tears, and her hair fell in disarray around her shoulders. But deep within her, a spark of hope flickered. She straightened her shoulders and smoothed her dress, determined to face whatever came next with grace and courage.

The path to Nathaniel's studio felt longer than usual, each step heavy with uncertainty. But as she approached, she could hear the soft sounds of paintbrushes against canvas, a familiar and comforting rhythm.

Taking a deep breath, she knocked gently on the door. There was a moment of silence before Nathaniel's voice called out, filled with surprise. "Elena?"

"Yes," she replied, her voice steady despite the pounding of her heart.

He opened the door, and their eyes met—hers, filled with vulnerability and longing; his, shadowed by the weight of their shared pain. "I didn't expect to see you," he said softly, stepping aside to let her in.

The studio was warm and filled with the scents of paint and turpentine. The sunlight streamed through the windows, casting a golden hue across the room, illuminating the canvases that adorned the walls. They were vibrant and alive, starkly contrasting the heavy atmosphere that lingered between them.

"I've been thinking," Elena began, her heart racing. "About us, about everything. I can't keep running from this... from you."

Nathaniel's expression softened, the tension in his shoulders easing slightly. "I've been thinking about you too, Elena. About what happened. I never meant for it to come between us."

"I know," she replied, stepping closer. "But we can't let the past define our future. Our love is worth fighting for, despite the history that weighs on us."

Nathaniel's eyes flickered with hope, but doubt still lingered in his gaze. "What if we can't escape it? What if the curse is stronger than our love?"

Elena reached out, taking his hand in hers. The warmth of his skin ignited a spark of determination within her. "We have to try. We can uncover the truth together. We can break this cycle."

She could see the conflict in his eyes, the battle between fear and hope. But as he looked down at their intertwined hands, she saw the flicker of resolve beginning to burn brighter. "You're right. I don't want to lose you, Elena. We can't let our ancestors' mistakes dictate our fate."

Together, they took a tentative step forward, their hearts syncing once more. The wall that had separated them was not yet fully dismantled, but it was beginning to crack under the weight of their shared determination.

"I want to understand this curse," Elena continued, her voice steady. "I want to know what we're up against so that we can confront it. I don't want to hide from it any longer."

Nathaniel nodded, his expression shifting to one of commitment. "Then let's do it. We'll explore every avenue, uncover every secret. Together."

With their hearts aligned, they began to talk—about the curse, their fears, and their hopes. The barriers that had once seemed insurmountable began to dissolve as they shared their vulnerabilities, and Elena felt the warmth of their connection rekindling like the first rays of dawn breaking through the night.

As the sun dipped below the horizon, casting a warm glow over the studio, they forged a pact to face the unknown together. In that moment, the shadows that had threatened to consume them began to recede, replaced by the promise of healing and a renewed bond forged in love.

They stood side by side, united in their resolve, ready to confront the darkness of the past and illuminate a path toward a future free from the shackles of fear and despair. Together, they would rise from the ashes of heartbreak and embrace the healing power of love—a love that was destined to thrive despite the storms that lay ahead.

20

The Heart's Resurgence Whispers of Hope

Spring breathed new life into Hawthorn Hill, the once-gray estate now alive with the colors of blooming flowers and the sounds of nature awakening from its winter slumber. The world outside mirrored the shift within Elena's heart—one that had begun to thaw after the ice of heartbreak and uncertainty.

In the wake of her reconciliation with Nathaniel, she felt the stirrings of hope, but the path to healing remained unclear. It was during a visit to the village that fate intervened in the form of an old family friend, Mrs. Beatrice Lovelace, a woman whose wisdom and warmth had always enveloped Elena like a favorite shawl.

Mrs. Lovelace was a vibrant woman, her silver hair pulled back in a loose bun, with twinkling eyes that seemed to hold the secrets of the universe. She had been a companion to Elena's grandmother, a stalwart presence in the Hawthorne family, and often spoke of the importance of art in overcoming personal struggles.

"Ah, my dear Elena!" she exclaimed, embracing her tightly. "It warms my heart to see you. You've been missed in the village. I heard about the storm that swept through Hawthorn Hill. You must come and visit more often; the world needs your light!"

Elena smiled, but her heart felt heavy. "Thank you, Mrs. Lovelace. I've been... finding my way through some things."

As they settled into the cozy parlor of Mrs. Lovelace's cottage, surrounded by shelves brimming with books and an array of colorful paintings, the older woman poured them both cups of herbal tea, its fragrant aroma filling the air.

"Now, tell me everything," Mrs. Lovelace urged, her eyes sparkling with curiosity. "I know you have much on your mind. Is it love that troubles you?"

Elena hesitated, glancing down at her hands, which cradled the warm cup. "It's complicated," she admitted. "Nathaniel and I... we found our way back to each other, but the shadows of our families loom large over us. There's a curse that has plagued my lineage for generations, and I fear it will consume us."

Mrs. Lovelace's expression shifted, her brows knitting together with concern. "Curses are but the manifestations of our fears and the burdens we carry. They can be broken, my dear. What is it you truly desire?"

"I want to break free from the past," Elena said, her voice trembling. "I want to find hope and a way forward. I've lost my passion for art, and I don't know how to reclaim it."

A gentle smile spread across Mrs. Lovelace's face. "Ah, art is the language of the heart! It holds the power to heal, to express the unspoken and to uncover the hidden. You must reconnect with it, dear girl. You must allow your heart to speak again."

Elena felt a flicker of excitement at the thought. Memories of her childhood flooded back—of painting in the sun-drenched gardens, of losing herself in colors and shapes, of feeling as though she could transcend the weight of her family's history. "But where do I start?" she asked, feeling a blend of hope and trepidation.

"Start small," Mrs. Lovelace advised, her voice soothing. "Find a canvas and let your emotions flow freely. Don't worry about the outcome; allow yourself to feel and express without judgment. Art is not merely about perfection; it is about the journey of self-discovery."

Encouraged by Mrs. Lovelace's wisdom, Elena made her way back to Hawthorn Hill with a renewed sense of purpose. She ventured into the old studio that had once belonged to her mother, dust motes dancing in the sunlight that streamed through the windows. The room felt like a sanctuary, filled with the scent of linseed oil and the remnants of unfinished canvases.

With every brushstroke, she felt a resurgence of emotion—joy, sorrow, longing. The colors began to blend and swirl on the canvas, each hue an expression of the tangled feelings within her. She painted not only for herself but for her ancestors, for the women who had endured the burden of love and loss before her.

Days turned into weeks as she immersed herself in her art, and the act of creation became her solace. She explored landscapes of her dreams, painted portraits of family members whose gazes seemed to urge her on, and captured the vibrant essence of life that pulsed outside the estate's walls.

One afternoon, while engrossed in her work, Nathaniel entered the studio quietly, his presence like a soft whisper in the air. Elena turned to him, paintbrush poised mid-air, surprise flickering in her eyes.

"Nathaniel," she said, her heart racing. "I didn't expect you."

"I wanted to see you," he replied, stepping closer, a mixture of apprehension and admiration in his gaze. "I heard you were painting again. I needed to witness it for myself."

Elena smiled shyly, feeling a warmth bloom in her chest. "It's been... healing. I'm trying to express everything I've been feeling."

As he examined the canvas, the weight of his gaze ignited something within her. "It's beautiful," he said, his voice barely above a whisper. "You have such a gift, Elena."

The compliment warmed her soul, and she felt a surge of confidence. "It's not just about the art, though. It's about reclaiming my joy, my voice. I want to break free from the shadows."

Nathaniel's expression softened, and he stepped closer, his hand brushing against hers, sending a spark through her. "You're doing it, you know. You're breaking free, and I want to be part of that journey."

Encouraged by his words, Elena felt her heart swell. "I want that too, Nathaniel. I want us to move forward, to face the curse together, but I need to find my footing first."

He nodded, understanding evident in his eyes. "Then let's support each other. We'll explore the history and the curse together, but we'll also nurture our passions. We can create something beautiful out of this mess."

As they spoke, the air around them filled with a renewed sense of possibility. Together, they could navigate the intricacies of their shared past while nurturing the present. The whispers of hope began to drown out the fears that had once held them captive.

Elena picked up her paintbrush and gestured to a blank canvas. "Would you like to join me? We can create something together—a testament to our journey."

Nathaniel hesitated for a moment before a smile broke across his face. "I'd love that."

With laughter bubbling between them, Nathaniel picked up a brush and dipped it into a vibrant blue paint, his strokes tentative yet determined. They painted side by side, their laughter blending with the colors on the canvas—a beautiful collaboration born from the ashes of their past.

As they worked together, Elena felt a surge of gratitude for the love that had survived amidst the storms. With every brushstroke, they were not just expressing their individual passions but weaving their dreams together into something greater.

The heart's resurgence was not merely about healing; it was a celebration of love, resilience, and the promise of new beginnings. In the warmth of the studio, surrounded by the vibrancy of their art, Elena knew that they could rewrite their story—a tale of hope and courage that would echo through the generations.

As the sun dipped below the horizon, casting golden light across the canvas, Elena felt the darkness that had once enveloped her begin to lift. With Nathaniel by her side, she embraced the whispers of hope that danced in the air—a promise that together, they could transcend the past and create a future filled with love, joy, and endless possibilities.

21

A Reunion of Souls Fateful Encounters

The winds of change swept over Hawthorn Hill, rustling the leaves of the ancient oaks that bordered the estate. The air crackled with anticipation, a promise of new beginnings, as Nathaniel Grey approached the towering front doors of the home that had become both a refuge and a battlefield for his heart.

It had been weeks since he and Elena had shared that afternoon in the studio, painting their hopes and dreams side by side. In that time, Nathaniel had been grappling with his emotions, the weight of their families' history pressing down on him like a storm cloud. The ache of separation from Elena felt unbearable, a constant reminder of what he had nearly lost.

He had spent his days wandering the picturesque Yorkshire countryside, seeking solace in the rolling hills and serene landscapes. Each moment away from Elena had intensified his longing, making it clear that she was not just a fleeting connection but the very essence of his soul's desire. It was time to confront the fears that had kept them apart and reclaim the love that had blossomed amidst the shadows of their shared history.

Drawing a deep breath, he pushed open the heavy door of Hawthorn Hill. The familiar scent of aged wood and lilac lingered in the air, and the soft echo of his footsteps on the polished floor felt like a welcoming embrace. But as he stepped inside, he also felt the weight of the estate's history bearing down on him—the secrets that lingered in every corner, the echoes of voices long gone.

"Elena?" he called, his voice reverberating through the grand hall. The silence that followed felt oppressive, wrapping around him like a thick fog. He had been so sure that she would be there, lost in her art or perhaps wandering the gardens that had once inspired her as a child.

Just as doubt began to creep in, he heard a soft voice from the drawing room. "In here!"

His heart raced as he made his way down the hall, a blend of hope and apprehension swirling within him. The drawing room was warm and inviting, the sunlight pouring through the large windows, illuminating the space with a golden glow. And there, seated on the plush settee, was Elena.

She looked up as he entered, and for a moment, the world around them faded away. The sight of her, with her hair cascading softly over her shoulders and her eyes sparkling with a mix of surprise and uncertainty, ignited a fire within him.

"Nathaniel," she breathed, rising to her feet, a mixture of joy and trepidation flickering across her face. "I didn't expect you."

"I had to see you," he replied, stepping closer. "I've missed you, Elena. Every moment apart felt like an eternity. I'm here to fight for us."

Her gaze softened, and for a brief moment, the shadows that had clouded their connection seemed to lift. "I've missed you too, but things are complicated. The weight of our families' histories feels heavier than ever."

"I know," he said, his voice steady. "But I believe we can overcome it. Together. We've already started to break the chains that bind us."

Elena looked down, her fingers fidgeting with the hem of her dress. "It's just that I'm scared. Scared that the past will come back to haunt us. Scared that we'll hurt each other."

Nathaniel reached out, gently lifting her chin so that their eyes met. "I understand that fear, but I refuse to let it control us. We're not our families' mistakes, and we don't have to carry their burdens alone. Let's face the truth together and uncover what's been hidden."

Elena's breath caught in her throat, the intensity of his gaze stirring something deep within her. The winds outside howled, swirling leaves in a frenzy, as if echoing the tempest of emotions brewing between them.

"Promise me we can explore this together," he continued, his voice a soothing balm against her uncertainty. "Let's confront the curse, the past, everything that stands in our way."

Tears brimmed in Elena's eyes, her heart swelling with longing. "I want that, Nathaniel. I want you. But how do we begin?"

He took her hands in his, feeling the warmth of her skin against his. "Let's start with what we know. We can uncover the history of our families, the truth behind the curse that has haunted us. I want to understand everything, and I want you by my side."

A sense of determination ignited within her as she nodded, the flicker of hope returning. "Yes, let's do it. Together."

With their hands intertwined, they stood at the precipice of a journey that would lead them deep into the heart of Hawthorn Hill's secrets. The winds outside picked up, howling against the windows as if urging them onward, and in that moment, Elena felt the weight of the past begin to lift, replaced by the strength of their renewed bond.

"Let's start with the library," Nathaniel suggested, his eyes alight with enthusiasm. "Your family has kept records, stories that might reveal more about this curse. Perhaps there are clues to break it."

Elena felt a thrill run through her at the thought of uncovering the truth. "Yes! My grandmother used to tell me stories of our family, of those who came before. She had a particular interest in the Hawthorne legacy and the tragedies that befell us. There might be something hidden in the archives."

As they made their way through the grand halls of the estate, their footsteps echoed like a heartbeat—a steady rhythm propelling them forward into the unknown. The library stood at the end of the corridor, its imposing oak doors a gateway to knowledge and history.

As they entered, Elena was enveloped in the familiar scent of old books and polished wood. She felt a sense of reverence wash over her as she gazed at the shelves lined with volumes filled with the stories of her ancestors.

Nathaniel moved to her side, and together they began to explore, their fingers brushing against the spines of books as they searched for answers. "What are we looking for?" he asked, his curiosity piqued.

"Anything that mentions the curse or our family's history," Elena replied, her heart racing with anticipation. "My grandmother mentioned a journal that contained secrets about our lineage. It was said to be hidden in the library."

As they began to sift through the books, a sense of purpose enveloped them. With each volume they pulled from the shelves, they drew closer to unraveling the mysteries that had haunted their families for generations.

Hours passed as they searched, laughter mingling with moments of silence, both lost in the journey of discovery. They uncovered tales of love and loss, of dreams that had been dashed against the rocks of fate. Elena felt the threads of her ancestry weaving through her as she learned about the strength and resilience of the women in her family, each one echoing the passions and struggles she felt within her own heart.

Finally, just as they were beginning to feel the weight of despair settle over them, Nathaniel's voice broke through the silence. "Elena! Look at this."

He held up a dusty, leather-bound journal, its cover worn with age but still bearing the insignia of the Hawthorne family crest. Elena's heart raced as she took the book from him, brushing away the dust to reveal the intricate patterns etched into the leather.

"This is it," she breathed, her voice trembling with excitement. "This must be my grandmother's journal."

With trembling hands, she opened the journal, and the pages seemed to whisper secrets of the past. Together, they poured over the entries, each word illuminating the shadows of their shared history.

As they read about the heartbreaks and triumphs of her ancestors, Elena felt the burdens of the past begin to lift. They uncovered stories of forbidden love, of choices made in the name of family loyalty, and of the curse that had loomed like a specter over their lineage. Each revelation brought them closer together, solidifying their resolve to break free from the chains of history.

"Look here," Nathaniel said, pointing to a passage written in her grandmother's elegant script. "It speaks of a ritual, a way to confront the curse directly. It mentions the power of love and unity."

Elena's heart raced as she read the words aloud. "It says that only through understanding and forgiveness can the curse be lifted. Love must conquer the shadows that bind us."

Hope surged within her, intertwining with the resolve that had taken root in her heart. "This is it, Nathaniel. This is our way forward!"

As they closed the journal, the winds outside began to howl once more, the storm rising in intensity. But inside the library, a sense of calm enveloped them, as if the very walls of Hawthorn Hill were urging them onward.

With newfound determination, Elena turned to Nathaniel, her eyes shining with purpose. "We will face this together, and we will break this curse. The shadows of our families will no longer dictate our futures."

He smiled, the warmth of his gaze igniting a spark of courage within her. "Yes, together. We'll rewrite our story."

Hand in hand, they stepped away from the library, ready to face the challenges ahead. The winds of change were swirling around them once more, but this time, they felt equipped to embrace whatever storms may come.

As they walked through the halls of Hawthorn Hill, they felt the echoes of their ancestors guiding them, the whispers of hope intertwining with the love that had sparked between them. Together, they would rewrite their fate, their souls entwined in a dance of love and resilience, forever determined to break the cycle of despair.

22

Secrets Revealed Unmasking the Truth

The air inside Hawthorn Hill felt charged with anticipation as Elena and Nathaniel prepared to face the truths that had been buried beneath layers of family secrets and heartache. The journal lay open on the ornate wooden table in the drawing room, its pages filled with the echoes of their ancestors' lives and the curse that had haunted the Hawthorne lineage for generations.

Elena took a deep breath, her heart racing. "We need to discuss what we've uncovered in the journal, Nathaniel," she began, her voice steady despite the storm of emotions swirling within her. "If we're going to confront this curse, we need to be honest with each other."

Nathaniel nodded, his expression serious. "I agree. There are things I've kept hidden from you, things that could change everything."

Elena felt a twinge of anxiety at his words. "And I, too, have secrets that weigh on my heart. It's time we unmask the truth—no more shadows between us."

As they sat across from each other, the light from the flickering fireplace cast dancing shadows on the walls, echoing the uncertainties that loomed over their relationship.

"What's been troubling you?" Nathaniel asked, his gaze penetrating as he studied her face.

Elena hesitated, then spoke slowly, her voice barely above a whisper. "When I returned to Hawthorn Hill, I discovered more about my family's history than I had anticipated. I learned about the women who came before me—about their passions, their regrets, and the love affairs that ended in tragedy. It was as if I was living their stories, caught in a web of desires that couldn't be fulfilled."

Nathaniel leaned closer, his eyes softening. "That must have been difficult for you. But you're not bound by their choices, Elena. You have the power to create your own destiny."

Elena nodded, her heart swelling at his encouragement. "But that's not all. I've been haunted by the notion that our families' pasts could intertwine in ways we never imagined." She took a deep breath, steeling herself for what she was about to reveal. "I found a letter addressed to my grandmother, written by a man named Edward Grey. He claimed to be deeply in love with a Hawthorne woman, and I suspect that he's part of your family."

Nathaniel's expression shifted, a mix of surprise and concern flashing across his features. "Edward Grey? He was my great-uncle. I've heard whispers about his relationship with a Hawthorne woman, but the details were always vague."

"Vague enough to be dangerous," Elena said, her voice tightening. "What if that relationship was the catalyst for the curse? What if their love was doomed from the start?"

The weight of her words hung heavy in the air as Nathaniel considered the implications. "If they were indeed star-crossed lovers, that could explain the turmoil that has plagued our families for generations. But there's something else I've been keeping from you—something about my own family's past."

Elena felt a knot of apprehension tighten in her stomach. "What is it?"

"My family has a history of tragedy connected to the Hawthorne name," Nathaniel confessed, his voice low. "I never wanted to burden you with it, but my mother told me stories of her family's dealings with the Hawthornes and how love could tear lives apart. They lost everything—status, wealth, happiness—over that relationship. They always said the curse would come for the Greys next."

Elena's heart raced as the pieces began to fall into place. "So, we're not just victims of our families' histories; we're also part of a cycle that has repeated itself through generations."

"Yes," Nathaniel said, his eyes filled with regret. "And I fear that our love might be the final chapter in this tragic tale."

A silence fell between them, heavy with the weight of their revelations. The flickering flames cast ominous shadows across the room, and Elena felt the chill of fear creeping into her heart. Could their love truly be cursed?

"What if we're meant to break this cycle?" she suggested, her voice trembling yet resolute. "What if our love is strong enough to conquer the shadows? We've already started by confronting the truth together."

Nathaniel's gaze met hers, and in that moment, she saw the fierce determination mirrored in his eyes. "You're right. We can't let the past dictate our future. But we need to understand the full extent of the curse if we're going to confront it."

Elena nodded, emboldened by his strength. "The journal spoke of a ritual, but it didn't provide many details. We need to delve deeper into the history of our families and find a way to honor those who came before us while forging our own path."

Nathaniel stood, his expression resolute. "Let's make it our mission. We'll search for more information—visit the village archives, talk to the elders, do whatever it takes to uncover the truth. Together."

As he spoke, the winds howled outside, the storm intensifying. Elena felt a rush of excitement mingled with fear. This journey would not be easy, but they were ready to face whatever came their way.

Suddenly, a loud crash echoed from outside, rattling the windows. Elena jumped, her heart racing. "What was that?"

"Probably just the storm," Nathaniel replied, though his eyes reflected concern. "But we should check it out."

They moved toward the door, the anticipation building as they stepped outside into the tempest. The wind whipped around them, chilling their skin as they made their way toward the source of the noise.

As they rounded the corner of the house, they gasped at the sight before them. A large tree had fallen, its branches splintered and debris scattered across the ground. But beneath the tree's shattered form lay something unexpected—a weathered wooden box, partially buried in the earth.

"What is that?" Elena asked, her curiosity piqued as she approached the box.

Nathaniel knelt beside it, brushing away the dirt and debris to reveal intricate carvings etched into the wood. "I don't know, but it looks old. It could be connected to our families."

Heart racing, Elena knelt beside him, her fingers tracing the carvings. "Should we open it?"

Nathaniel hesitated, a flicker of uncertainty crossing his face. "It could hold more secrets—perhaps the very answers we've been seeking."

"Or it could be a warning," Elena said softly, her voice filled with trepidation. "But we can't turn back now. We need to know what lies inside."

With a shared glance of determination, they pried open the box, the hinges creaking in protest as they lifted the lid. Inside, they found a collection of aged letters, sepia-toned photographs, and what appeared to be an ornate locket.

Elena gasped, her fingers trembling as she lifted the locket. "This belonged to my grandmother! I've seen it in portraits of her."

Nathaniel picked up one of the letters, his brow furrowing as he scanned the faded ink. "These are love letters—written between your grandmother and Edward Grey."

Elena's heart pounded in her chest. "What do they say?"

With a mixture of awe and trepidation, Nathaniel began to read aloud. "My dearest Eleanor, every moment spent apart is a moment filled with despair... I long for the day when our families can see our love for what it truly is—an unbreakable bond that transcends the darkness that seeks to keep us apart."

As he continued to read, the atmosphere thickened with the weight of their ancestors' emotions. The letters spoke of secret meetings, stolen glances, and a love so fierce it defied the conventions of their time.

"I had no idea," Elena whispered, tears welling in her eyes. "This is a part of my family's history I never knew. It's as if they were living in the shadows, just as we have."

"Your grandmother loved him," Nathaniel said softly, his voice laced with emotion. "This love was real, yet it was suffocated by the burdens of their families' legacies."

As they pored over the letters, the revelations began to unfurl like a tapestry woven with threads of desire, betrayal, and ultimately, heartbreak. Each letter carried the weight of dreams unrealized and the anguish of unfulfilled love.

Finally, they reached the last letter, the ink smudged with tears. "I fear the path we tread is fraught with danger," Nathaniel read, his voice thick with emotion. "But love cannot be extinguished, even in the face of the greatest adversity. We must hold onto hope, for it is the only light in the darkness."

Elena felt the tears spill over, the emotions crashing over her like waves. "They were willing to fight for their love, Nathaniel. It's as if they were leaving us a message—an invitation to break free from the shackles of our families' pasts."

Nathaniel's gaze met hers, the determination in his eyes burning bright. "Then we will honor them. We will not let fear dictate our fate. We will fight for our love, just as they did."

With renewed strength, they stood together, united in purpose. The storm raged around them, but inside their hearts, a fire ignited—a fierce, unyielding love that would not be swayed by the darkness of the past.

Hand in hand, they returned to the safety of Hawthorn Hill, ready to uncover more secrets and face whatever challenges lay ahead. As they stepped inside, the echoes of their ancestors whispered in the air, a reminder that love, despite its trials, was always worth fighting for.

Together, Elena and Nathaniel would forge their own path, unmasking the truth and breaking the cycle of despair that had plagued their families for generations. The storm outside continued to howl, but inside, they found solace in each other—a bond unbreakable and a love destined to conquer the shadows.

23

The Dance of Fate Steps to Destiny

The grand ballroom of Hawthorn Hill was alive with music and laughter, the rich melodies of a string quartet echoing off the high, ornately carved ceilings. Chandeliers sparkled above like stars trapped in glass, casting shimmering light across the sea of elegantly dressed guests. Gowns of satin and silk swirled around them, while men in tailored suits exchanged polite conversation, their laughter mingling with the symphony of joy and celebration.

Elena Hawthorne stood at the edge of the ballroom, her breath catching in her throat as she took in the lavish spectacle before her. It had been years since a ball had graced Hawthorn Hill, and tonight felt like a turning point—a chance to embrace her heritage while daring to create her own destiny.

But her heart was not wholly in the celebration. It was pulled in another direction, towards the brooding figure of Nathaniel Grey, who stood across the room, his dark eyes scanning the crowd. He looked dashing in his tailored suit, yet a hint of storm clouds lingered in his expression. She could see the conflict etched across his features, as if he were grappling with some inner turmoil that threatened to overshadow the evening's festivities.

As their eyes met, an electric spark ignited between them, and the world around them faded into a blur. A warm smile broke across Nathaniel's face, momentarily dispelling the shadows that had darkened his gaze. He moved toward her, weaving through the crowd like a ship navigating through a tempest. Elena's heart raced with anticipation, a mixture of longing and apprehension churning within her.

"Elena," he said, his voice low and rich, sending shivers down her spine. "You look breathtaking tonight."

"Thank you, Nathaniel," she replied, her cheeks warming under his gaze. "You look quite handsome yourself."

Just then, the music swelled, and the floor cleared for the opening dance. Elena felt a flutter of excitement mixed with anxiety as the guests turned their attention to the couple who would lead the first dance. They stepped into the center of the room, their hands brushing against each other in a lingering touch, the connection palpable.

"Shall we?" Nathaniel extended his hand, his eyes glimmering with a challenge. She placed her hand in his, feeling the warmth radiate from his touch. The world melted away as they took their first steps together, moving to the rhythm of the music.

As they danced, the elegance of the ballroom enveloped them, each movement a graceful testament to their rekindled bond. The swirl of their bodies mirrored the tempest of their emotions, a blend of passion, uncertainty, and hope. Nathaniel pulled her closer, their bodies fitting together like pieces of a puzzle, and in that moment, the past and its burdens faded away.

"I've missed this," Nathaniel said, his voice barely above a whisper as they twirled beneath the sparkling chandeliers. "Being with you. The world seems brighter when you're near."

Elena's heart soared at his words, but she could sense the weight of unspoken fears lurking just beneath the surface. "But what about the secrets? The history that could tear us apart?"

He hesitated, his brow furrowing. "We can't let the past dictate our future. We have to believe that our love is stronger than the legacies we inherit."

As they continued to dance, Elena felt the gazes of the guests around them. Some looked on with admiration, while others whispered amongst themselves, their expressions betraying a mix of intrigue and judgment. She couldn't shake the feeling that their love was a spectacle—enthralling yet vulnerable to the scrutiny of those who had long held onto the weight of tradition and expectation.

Suddenly, a figure moved through the crowd, a striking woman in a striking crimson gown. Elena's heart sank as she recognized Lady Margaret, Nathaniel's mother, her expression a mixture of disdain and determination.

"Ah, Nathaniel, there you are," Lady Margaret called out, her voice cutting through the melodic strains of the music. The crowd parted for her, eyes darting toward the impending confrontation. "I was looking for you. I'd like a word."

Nathaniel's grip on Elena tightened, his brow darkening. "Not now, Mother," he said, his tone firm yet strained.

"Don't be foolish, Nathaniel. This is not the time to indulge in fantasies," Lady Margaret insisted, her voice cool and commanding. "We need to discuss your future, and I will not have you wasting it on this—this distraction."

Elena felt her heart sink as she stepped back, the warmth of their connection instantly evaporating in the face of his mother's cold demeanor.

"Mother, I—" Nathaniel began, but Lady Margaret interrupted him, her sharp gaze fixed on Elena.

"Really, Nathaniel? You've chosen to dance with *her*?" Lady Margaret's voice dripped with condescension. "Do you truly believe this will lead to anything meaningful?"

"Lady Margaret," Elena interjected, her voice steady despite the storm brewing inside her. "Nathaniel and I share a bond that transcends our families' pasts. It is real, and it matters."

"Real?" Lady Margaret scoffed, her laughter ringing like a bell of judgment. "Your family's name is steeped in scandal. Do you not see the folly in this? The Hawthorne curse is not a myth, my dear. It is a reality, and it has taken down families before. You cannot think that you and Nathaniel can escape its grasp."

The tension in the air thickened as murmurs rippled through the gathered guests, their interest piqued by the confrontation. Elena felt exposed, the weight of scrutiny pressing down on her.

"Nathaniel, you deserve a future without the baggage of her family's dark history," Lady Margaret continued, her voice rising with urgency. "You can still make something of yourself—someone of significance—if you let go of this fleeting whim."

Elena could see Nathaniel's resolve waver as he glanced between his mother and her, torn between the love he felt for her and the obligations he had been raised to uphold.

"Mother, please," Nathaniel pleaded, his voice strained. "Elena is not a whim. She's a part of me, and I will not let you dictate my life any longer."

With those words, a silence enveloped the room, the tension palpable as the guests watched in rapt attention. Elena's heart swelled with pride, but fear clawed at her insides. Would their love be strong enough to withstand the storm?

"Nathaniel," Lady Margaret said, her voice dropping to a dangerous whisper, "if you pursue this relationship, you will lose everything—your family's support, your future, your very name."

A hush fell over the crowd, anticipation crackling in the air like static. Nathaniel looked deeply into Elena's eyes, and for a moment, it felt as though the world had paused.

"I'm willing to risk it all for you," he declared, his voice filled with conviction. "I refuse to let fear and obligation dictate my choices any longer."

The ballroom erupted into a mixture of gasps and whispers as Lady Margaret recoiled, shock painted across her features. Elena felt a surge of hope and fear intertwine, realizing that this moment would define their love story forever.

"Very well, Nathaniel," Lady Margaret spat, her tone venomous. "You will regret this decision. Mark my words." With that, she turned on her heel and stormed out of the ballroom, the tension thickening as she left behind an uneasy silence.

Elena breathed deeply, the weight of the world feeling lighter in Nathaniel's presence. "Are you sure about this?" she asked, her voice trembling with both exhilaration and fear.

"I've never been more certain about anything," Nathaniel replied, his grip tightening around her waist, pulling her close. "Let the world say what they will. We will forge our own path."

With the music swelling once more, they resumed their dance, the world around them fading into insignificance as they moved together in a rhythm that felt both exhilarating and terrifying. Each step, each twirl, ignited a passion that pulsed through their veins, a reminder that love, in all its forms, was worth fighting for.

The winds outside howled with renewed vigor, a reflection of the tumult within them, but in the heart of Hawthorn Hill, amid the laughter and elegance, Elena and Nathaniel danced defiantly against the tide of fate. Together, they would face whatever challenges lay ahead, stepping boldly into the unknown—a dance of destiny that could not be broken.

24

The Final Confrontation Clash of Hearts

The storm outside raged like a tempest unleashed, dark clouds swirling overhead, mirroring the turmoil that churned within Elena Hawthorne. The walls of Hawthorn Hill seemed to tremble as the winds howled, a cacophony of nature that reflected the chaos of her heart. After the ball, the sense of exhilaration she had felt faded, replaced by an overwhelming sense of urgency. Tonight, she would confront the legacy that had haunted her family for generations.

Elena stood at the foot of the grand staircase, the old oak bannister cold beneath her fingertips. The estate loomed around her, steeped in shadows and secrets, a silent witness to the battle she was about to wage. She had spent her life dancing in the shadows of her ancestors' choices, but now it was time to step into the light.

Nathaniel waited in the drawing room, the flickering flames of the fireplace casting his handsome features into sharp relief. He stood near a window, looking out at the storm that swept across the moors. As she entered, he turned, and their eyes locked. In that moment, the world outside faded away. Despite the raging storm, she could feel his unwavering support—a lifeline in the turmoil.

"Are you ready for this?" Nathaniel asked, his voice low but steady, his brow slightly furrowed with concern.

"I have to be," she replied, her voice firm yet tinged with uncertainty. "I can't let my family's past dictate my future. I won't let them control me any longer."

Elena took a deep breath, steeling herself. She had to confront her parents and the ghosts of her lineage—their mistakes, their fears, and their curses. The legacy that had once threatened to bind her now fueled her resolve. Together, they would stand against the tide.

With Nathaniel by her side, they made their way through the dimly lit corridors, each step echoing like a drumbeat of impending confrontation. The ancestral portraits lining the walls seemed to watch them, their painted eyes following every movement, as if they sensed the rebellion in Elena's heart.

As they approached the family library, a sanctuary of knowledge and tradition, Elena could hear the murmur of voices inside. She paused, her heart pounding in her chest, nerves threatening to overtake her.

"Remember, I'm right here with you," Nathaniel whispered, his hand resting gently on the small of her back, grounding her.

With a nod, she pushed open the heavy oak door, the creak of the hinges announcing their arrival. Inside, the room was bathed in a warm glow from the fireplace, casting flickering shadows that danced along the walls. Her parents, along with a few key family members, were gathered around a table laden with family documents—secrets of the past laid bare for all to see.

"Elena!" her mother exclaimed, startled. "What are you doing here?"

"I came to talk," Elena replied, her voice firm but her heart raced. She met her mother's gaze, steeling herself against the tidal wave of expectations that flooded the room. "I need to speak about Nathaniel."

Her father's expression hardened, eyes narrowing in disapproval. "This again? We've already had this discussion, Elena. Nathaniel Grey is not suitable for you."

"Not suitable?" she echoed, anger rising within her. "You don't even know him! You only see what you want to see—the family name, the legacy. But love isn't about names or legacies. It's about the person who stands beside you, and Nathaniel is that person for me."

"Love? You're talking about love?" her mother scoffed, rising from her seat, indignation written all over her face. "Do you have any idea what kind of trouble you're inviting into this family? The Hawthornes have always upheld a legacy of strength, and you want to throw it away for a fleeting passion?"

"Fleeting?" Elena's voice rang out, surprising herself with the strength behind it. "What I feel for Nathaniel is anything but fleeting. He's shown me a world beyond this cursed estate—a world where I can be free to choose my path."

The air in the room thickened with tension. Her father stood, hands clenched at his sides, a storm brewing in his own eyes. "You have no idea of the sacrifices our family has made, the burdens we carry. You think you can just turn your back on everything? On your heritage?"

"Maybe it's time to break the cycle!" Elena countered, feeling the weight of her family's expectations pressing down on her. "We've lived in the shadows of our ancestors' mistakes for too long! The curse that haunts us doesn't have to dictate our lives. We can choose love over fear, legacy over love."

As her words hung in the air, a moment of silence ensued. The fire crackled softly, breaking the tension momentarily, and Elena caught Nathaniel's gaze across the room. He gave her an encouraging nod, his expression a mixture of pride and admiration.

"Your choice to be with Nathaniel does not just affect you," her mother insisted, her voice trembling with emotion. "It affects all of us. Your decision carries weight—history, expectations. Can you truly bear that burden?"

"I would rather bear the weight of my own choices than live under the suffocating expectations of a legacy I didn't choose," Elena declared, her heart racing but her resolve solid. "Nathaniel and I want to build our future, not be shackled by the past."

"Is that what you truly want, Elena?" her father asked, a mixture of concern and curiosity softening his voice. "Are you willing to risk everything?"

"Yes," she replied without hesitation. "I'm willing to risk it all for love, for my happiness."

Her parents exchanged glances, a flicker of uncertainty passing between them. The storm outside raged on, but in that moment, the tempest within the room shifted, the air heavy with the promise of change.

Elena stepped forward, the distance between her and her parents closing. "I know I cannot erase our history, but I refuse to be defined by it. I will find my own path, one that honors my heart and the love I have for Nathaniel."

The weight of her words lingered in the air, the room falling into a hushed stillness. Slowly, she turned to Nathaniel, who stepped closer, taking her hand in his. Together, they faced her family, a united front against the storm.

"What do you say?" Nathaniel asked, his voice steady. "We can break this cycle. Together."

Her parents regarded them for a long moment, the silence stretching thin, and Elena's heart pounded with anticipation. Finally, her mother's shoulders slumped slightly, the fire within her dimming.

"We've always believed that family comes first," her mother said, her voice tinged with a mix of resignation and acceptance. "But maybe... just maybe... it's time to let go. To allow our children to forge their own destinies."

Elena's breath caught in her throat, a mixture of disbelief and hope flooding her senses. "You mean that?"

"Love is not a weakness," her father said quietly, his voice gravelly with emotion. "And perhaps we've been too rigid in our expectations. If you truly believe this is right for you, then we will support your choice."

Tears sprang to Elena's eyes as she realized the magnitude of what her parents were offering. "Thank you," she whispered, her voice thick with gratitude.

But just as relief washed over her, her mother continued, "However, be prepared. The road ahead will not be easy. The world outside is unforgiving, and we cannot shield you from the consequences of your choices."

"We are ready to face whatever comes our way," Nathaniel replied, his grip tightening around Elena's hand. "Together."

As they stood united, a soft breeze swept through the library, carrying with it a sense of new beginnings. The storm outside began to fade, the winds softening as the clouds parted slightly, allowing moonlight to filter through the tall windows.

In that moment, Elena felt an overwhelming sense of peace wash over her. She had faced her fears, stood up for love, and challenged her family's legacy head-on. Together with Nathaniel, she would chart a new course—one that embraced love, hope, and the promise of a brighter future.

As the moonlight bathed the room in silver, Elena knew that the storm had passed. They had weathered the tempest, and now, they would step boldly into the dawn of a new day—hand in hand, ready to forge their own destiny.

25

Embracing the Storm Love's Resilience

The first rumblings of thunder echoed across the Yorkshire moors as the sky darkened, heavy with impending rain. Elena stood at the window of her bedroom in Hawthorn Hill, gazing out at the churning clouds that rolled in like an army, ready to unleash their fury upon the world. She felt the storm's familiar pull, the excitement that always accompanied its arrival—a sense of renewal, of cleansing, of a fresh start.

Despite the tempest brewing outside, there was a warmth in her heart that overshadowed the dark clouds. After the confrontation with her family, Elena felt lighter, free from the weight of secrets and expectations that had long haunted her. Nathaniel's presence in her life was a balm to her soul, a reminder that love could conquer even the fiercest storms.

As she turned away from the window, she caught a glimpse of Nathaniel entering the room, his expression a mixture of concern and affection. He moved closer, wrapping his arms around her waist, pulling her into the safety of his embrace. She could feel the heat radiating from him, warding off the chill that lingered in the air.

"Another storm is upon us," he murmured, his voice low and soothing. "Do you think we should prepare for it, or should we embrace it?"

Elena leaned back against him, her heart racing at his words. "What do you mean?"

"Instead of shying away from what's coming, we can face it together," Nathaniel suggested, his breath warm against her ear. "Love is like the storm; it can be fierce and unpredictable, but it can also be beautiful and transformative. Let's not fear it—let's embrace it."

The thought resonated deep within her. For so long, she had lived in fear of the storms—both the literal ones that battered the estate and the emotional tempests that stirred within her. But Nathaniel was right. Love had weathered many storms, and now it was time to acknowledge that their love was resilient enough to withstand whatever challenges lay ahead.

"Let's embrace it," she replied, turning to face him, her eyes filled with determination. "Let's show the world that we can endure anything as long as we're together."

Nathaniel smiled, his gaze intense and filled with unwavering support. "Then let's make this storm our own. We'll take it head-on."

They made their way to the grand drawing room, where the expansive windows overlooked the moors. The wind howled, rattling the panes, and Elena felt a thrill of excitement course through her. She could hear the rain beginning to pelt against the glass, each drop a reminder of the energy and life swirling outside.

As they settled on a comfortable sofa by the fire, Elena leaned into Nathaniel's side, feeling his warmth envelop her. "What do you think it will be like?" she asked, her voice barely rising above the roar of the wind.

He considered her question for a moment before replying, "Like a dance. There will be moments of chaos and moments of stillness. But with every turn, we'll discover something new about ourselves and each other."

Elena closed her eyes, picturing the storm as a dance. She envisioned swirling winds lifting them, twirling them around, the rhythm of nature guiding their movements. It was exhilarating and terrifying, yet she couldn't help but feel a sense of freedom in the imagery.

"Let's make it our dance then," she said, opening her eyes and meeting his gaze. "Let's not just survive the storm; let's thrive in it."

"Agreed," Nathaniel replied, his eyes sparkling with mischief. "Let's take the first step."

As the storm raged outside, they turned to each other, their laughter ringing out like music against the backdrop of thunder. With every roll of the storm, their hearts beat in tandem, echoing the symphony of their love. Together, they were invincible, a force to be reckoned with.

Elena pulled away slightly and took Nathaniel's hands in hers, feeling the strength of his fingers entwined with her own. "Tell me what you want, Nathaniel. What do you see for us?"

He paused, a thoughtful look crossing his face. "I see us creating art together—capturing the storms and the calm, the love and the struggle. I see a life filled with passion, a home built on understanding and trust. And I see us, no matter what challenges come our way, always choosing each other."

His words stirred something deep within her. She could almost see it—a vivid future where their love could flourish, where storms wouldn't frighten them but rather inspire them to grow and evolve.

"I want that too," she said, her voice steady. "I want to create a life filled with color and emotion, where our love is a canvas painted with every shade of experience."

As they spoke, the storm intensified, the wind whipping around the estate like a wild animal unleashed. The shadows in the room danced, flickering in rhythm with the flames, casting an enchanting glow over their intertwined hands.

"Let's take this moment," Nathaniel suggested, rising to his feet and pulling Elena with him. "Let's dance."

"What? Here?" Elena laughed, caught off guard by his spontaneity.

"Why not? The storm is a reminder of our freedom. Let's celebrate our love in the midst of it all."

With that, Nathaniel twirled her into his arms, the movement flowing effortlessly as if they had rehearsed this moment a thousand times. They spun around the room, laughter mingling with the wind as the thunder crashed outside.

Elena felt alive, every heartbeat echoing the pulse of the storm. She didn't care that the rain lashed against the windows or that the wind howled in fury. In this moment, she was enveloped in the warmth of Nathaniel's embrace, a sanctuary against the chaos.

They danced as if the world outside had vanished, lost in a rhythm that was entirely their own. Each movement drew them closer, the connection between them solidifying with every twirl and dip. They embraced the storm, surrendering to its power while celebrating their love's resilience.

As the storm continued to rage on, Elena and Nathaniel's laughter filled the air, a beautiful counterpoint to the tempest outside. They were not merely surviving; they were thriving, weaving their love story amid the chaos, refusing to let anything dim the brightness of their bond.

Finally, breathless from their impromptu dance, they collapsed onto the sofa, laughter subsiding into a comfortable silence. Nathaniel's arm draped around her shoulders, and she nestled into him, feeling his heartbeat against her cheek.

"I think we just created our own magic," he murmured, glancing out at the wild storm.

Elena smiled, knowing he was right. The storm may be fierce, but they had embraced it, transformed it into something beautiful. And in that moment, she knew their love was more than enough to weather any storm that life might throw their way.

"Here's to embracing every storm," she said softly, raising an imaginary glass. "And to the resilience of our love."

"To us," Nathaniel replied, leaning down to press a gentle kiss to her forehead, sealing their promise with a warmth that spread through her like sunshine breaking through the clouds.

As the storm raged on outside, inside Hawthorn Hill, love flourished—undaunted and unyielding, a powerful force that would carry them through whatever lay ahead. Together, they would embrace each tempest, celebrating the beauty found in the heart of the storm.

26

The Path to Redemption Forging New Beginnings

The morning after the storm, Hawthorn Hill stood transformed, as if the tempest had scrubbed it clean. Sunlight streamed through the windows, illuminating the dust motes dancing in the air, casting a golden glow over the grand estate. Elena Hawthorne stood in the drawing room, a steaming cup of tea cradled in her hands, contemplating the future that lay before her.

The storm had felt like a cleansing, washing away the remnants of her family's troubled past and leaving a sense of clarity in its wake. Today, Elena was determined to take the first steps toward redeeming her family's legacy while forging her own path with Nathaniel by her side.

With renewed resolve, she stepped outside, the morning air crisp and invigorating. The grounds of Hawthorn Hill were dotted with puddles reflecting the bright blue sky, and the scent of fresh earth mingled with the lingering aroma of rain. As she walked, her thoughts drifted back to the stories she had unearthed—those of heartache, betrayal, and unfulfilled dreams that had plagued her ancestors.

What if she could rewrite those stories? What if she could turn the echoes of sorrow into a symphony of hope?

Her mind made up, Elena headed toward the garden, where she knew Nathaniel would be sketching, capturing the beauty of the world around them. He was always inspired by nature, finding the extraordinary in the simplest of things.

As she approached, she found him seated on a stone bench, pencil in hand, lost in the creation of a landscape. His brow furrowed in concentration, yet there was a soft smile on his lips—a reflection of the contentment that came from his art.

"Good morning, artist," she called, her voice breaking the tranquility of the scene.

Nathaniel looked up, his eyes lighting up as they met hers. "Good morning, Elena. I was just thinking about you. Your spirit seems to have weathered the storm quite well."

"I feel different today," she replied, moving closer. "Stronger, somehow. I want to do something meaningful—something that honors the past but also builds a new future."

Intrigued, he set his pencil down and turned to face her fully. "What do you have in mind?"

"I want to organize a community gathering at Hawthorn Hill," she began, excitement bubbling in her chest. "I want to invite the villagers, share stories, and create a space where everyone can come together. It's time to break down the walls that have separated us from our neighbors and our own history."

Nathaniel's expression softened as he considered her words. "You want to bring the community into the heart of your family's estate? That's a bold idea."

"It's time for healing—for both the estate and my family. We've held on to so many burdens for too long, and I want to show that Hawthorn Hill can be a place of joy and connection, not just sorrow and secrets."

A moment of silence passed between them, filled with unspoken understanding. Nathaniel reached for her hand, intertwining his fingers with hers. "You're right. This estate has the potential to become a sanctuary, a beacon of hope. And I'd be honored to help you bring your vision to life."

Elena beamed at his support, feeling a warmth spread through her. "Together, we can create a new legacy—one that celebrates love and resilience rather than pain and regret."

As they began to discuss plans, ideas flowed freely, each one sparking a sense of excitement and purpose. They envisioned art displays showcasing local talent, storytelling sessions where villagers could share their own histories, and a feast celebrating the bounty of the land. The goal was clear: to foster community and forge new connections, healing the rifts that had existed for too long.

Over the next few days, Elena poured her heart into organizing the gathering. She met with villagers, reached out to local artists, and spread the word about the event. Nathaniel helped her design flyers, his artistic touch transforming simple announcements into beautiful invitations. As their collaboration deepened, so did their love, blossoming amidst the shared goal of redemption.

When the day of the gathering finally arrived, excitement buzzed in the air. The grounds of Hawthorn Hill were adorned with flowers, colorful banners, and tables laden with food, each detail reflecting the vibrant spirit Elena sought to cultivate. The estate, once a fortress of secrets, was now a welcoming embrace, ready to welcome the community.

As villagers began to arrive, Elena felt a rush of nerves. Would they accept her? Would they forgive the past? But as the sun dipped low in the sky, painting the horizon with hues of orange and pink, she was greeted with warm smiles and heartfelt greetings. Laughter filled the air, mingling with the sweet scent of blooming flowers.

Nathaniel stood beside her, his presence a steadying force as they welcomed their guests. Together, they navigated the gathering, sharing stories and laughter, connecting the past with the present. Each interaction seemed to weave a thread of unity, breaking down the barriers that had long existed between the Hawthornes and the villagers.

As the sun set, Elena stood on a small stage, heart racing as she prepared to speak. She glanced at Nathaniel, who nodded encouragingly. Taking a deep breath, she addressed the crowd.

"Thank you all for being here today," she began, her voice steady despite her nerves. "Hawthorn Hill has always been a part of this community, but it has also held many secrets and sorrows. Today, we are forging a new beginning—a chance to redefine our legacy."

The crowd fell silent, eyes fixed on her as she continued. "I am committed to breaking the cycle of heartache that has haunted my family. Together, we can create a future filled with love, understanding, and hope."

A gentle wave of applause erupted, filling her with courage. "I invite each of you to share your stories, to connect with one another, and to find joy in our shared experiences. Let us build a community that thrives on love rather than fear."

As she stepped down, the atmosphere was electric with possibility. Conversations blossomed, and the air was filled with the sounds of laughter and music. Villagers mingled with the Hawthornes, sharing tales of their own struggles and triumphs, their lives intertwining in a way that had once seemed impossible.

Elena felt a sense of peace settle over her. She glanced at Nathaniel, who was animatedly discussing art with a group of young villagers, his passion infectious. He caught her eye and smiled, and in that moment, she knew they were on the right path.

As the night unfolded, Elena realized that this gathering was just the beginning. Together, she and Nathaniel had the power to reshape their family's legacy, to turn a history of heartache into one of resilience and hope.

As the stars twinkled above, she felt the weight of the past lift, replaced by the promise of a brighter future. This was not just a community gathering; it was a celebration of new beginnings—a testament to love's resilience in the face of adversity.

With Nathaniel by her side, Elena embraced the storm of change, confident that they would forge ahead, hand in hand, ready to face whatever came next. The path to redemption had begun, and she was ready to walk it, one step at a time.

27

The Last Echo
Endings and Beginnings

The sun rose over Hawthorn Hill, casting a soft golden light across the estate, illuminating the remnants of the gathering that had taken place the night before. Laughter still lingered in the air, mingling with the scent of morning dew and blooming flowers. Elena Hawthorne stood at her window, taking in the serene beauty that surrounded her, her heart swelling with hope.

It had been a week since the community gathering, and the energy of that day continued to resonate within her. The villagers' smiles, the stories shared, and the warmth of connections made had woven a tapestry of healing, creating a new narrative for her family and the estate. But amid the newfound joy, shadows of the past still clung to the edges of her mind.

Elena turned away from the window, feeling a familiar pull. She knew she needed to confront the last echoes of her family's mistakes to truly move forward. In her heart, she understood that healing was not just about celebrating new beginnings; it was also about recognizing and reconciling the past.

That afternoon, she invited Nathaniel to join her in the old library, a place that had long felt steeped in sorrow and secrets. Dust motes danced in the shafts of light that filtered through the tall windows, illuminating the rows of books that lined the walls. It was here, amidst the volumes of her family's history, that she hoped to find clarity.

"Are you ready for this?" Nathaniel asked gently, sensing the weight of her thoughts. He leaned against the doorframe, arms crossed, his expression a mix of concern and support.

Elena nodded, swallowing hard. "I think so. I need to understand what happened, to forgive them. Only then can we truly move on."

With a deep breath, she approached the desk where her grandmother's journal lay. The leather-bound book had been hidden for years, its pages filled with the burdens of their family's past. As she opened it, the scent of old paper and ink filled her senses, transporting her to a time when her ancestors walked these halls.

"What do you need from me?" Nathaniel asked, stepping closer, his presence a grounding force as she prepared to unearth the past.

"Just your support. I may find things that are difficult to hear, but I want to face them. I want to find closure."

Elena began to read aloud, her voice steady yet tinged with emotion. The words flowed from the pages, telling stories of love and loss, betrayal and regret. Each entry revealed her grandmother's struggles, her desires thwarted by family obligations, and the longing for a love that never flourished.

As Elena read, Nathaniel listened intently, his eyes locked on her face, absorbing every word as if it were a sacred truth. He could see the weight of history pressing down on her, and he felt an urge to comfort her, to remind her of the strength she had shown in facing her family's legacy.

Hours passed as they delved deeper into the journal, uncovering tales of feuds that had fractured the family and mistakes that had rippled through generations. With each revelation, Elena felt a growing sense of empathy toward her ancestors. They had been shaped by their circumstances, just as she was shaped by hers.

"This one…" she paused, her fingers trembling as she turned a page. "It's about a forbidden romance. My grandmother loved someone from a rival family—a love that was never allowed to blossom. It ended in heartbreak and resentment."

Nathaniel's gaze softened, and he stepped closer, placing a hand on her shoulder. "That's not your fault, Elena. It was their choice to allow that pain to define them."

"I know," she replied, tears glistening in her eyes. "But I want to break this cycle. I want to forgive them for their mistakes so that I can move forward with my own life."

He nodded, understanding the profound journey she was undertaking. "Forgiveness doesn't erase the past. It allows you to reclaim your future."

Taking a deep breath, Elena read the final entry aloud, her voice steady despite the tremor of emotion that threatened to overwhelm her. It spoke of a desperate plea for understanding, a desire to escape the suffocating weight of family expectations. Her grandmother had wished for a love that would transcend the barriers imposed upon her—a wish that echoed in Elena's own heart.

As she finished, silence enveloped the room. The weight of the past hung in the air, but with it came a newfound clarity. Elena felt a sense of release, as if the very act of confronting these ghosts had dimmed their power over her.

"Thank you for being here with me," she said, looking up at Nathaniel, her heart swelling with gratitude. "This means more than you know."

He smiled softly, brushing a strand of hair behind her ear. "You're not alone in this, Elena. You're forging a new path, one that honors the past while embracing the future. Together, we can rewrite the story."

With a renewed sense of purpose, Elena felt the echoes of her family's mistakes begin to fade. She could see the outlines of a new beginning taking shape, one filled with love and forgiveness rather than sorrow and regret.

"I want to create something beautiful," she said, a fire igniting in her eyes. "A project that honors our history but also looks toward the future. A community mural, perhaps—a tapestry of our stories, our hopes, and our dreams."

Nathaniel's face lit up with enthusiasm. "That's a wonderful idea! We can invite everyone to contribute, to share their own stories and create something that reflects our community's spirit."

Elena nodded, envisioning the mural coming to life—a vibrant testament to resilience and unity, a blending of histories into something magnificent. "It will symbolize our journey toward healing and redemption."

As they began brainstorming ideas for the mural, Elena felt the last echoes of her family's past slip away, replaced by a sense of empowerment and hope. The path to redemption was not a solitary journey; it was a shared experience, filled with love and support.

With Nathaniel at her side, she knew they could create something beautiful that would resonate through the ages. Together, they would embrace the lessons of the past while forging a new legacy, one that celebrated love, forgiveness, and the power of community.

As they stood together in the old library, surrounded by the remnants of a storied past, Elena felt a sense of peace wash over her. The final echoes of their families' mistakes were fading, making way for a bright new beginning—a canvas ready to be filled with color, joy, and the promise of a shared future.

And with that, the journey toward redemption truly began.

28

Winds of Change
New Horizons

The air was crisp and invigorating as Elena Hawthorne and Nathaniel Grey stood on the crest of Hawthorn Hill, the estate sprawling behind them like a tapestry woven from their family's history. The clouds drifted lazily overhead, carrying whispers of change, and the scent of earth and blooming wildflowers filled the air. Today was not just a day like any other; it marked the beginning of their journey into the unknown—a journey filled with promise and the exhilarating thrill of newfound love.

Elena took a deep breath, allowing the fresh air to fill her lungs, feeling alive in a way she hadn't for years. It was time to leave the weight of the past behind, to embrace the winds of change that were beckoning them toward a brighter future.

"We're really doing this," she said, her voice a mix of disbelief and excitement. She turned to Nathaniel, who stood beside her, a steadfast presence against the backdrop of the expansive landscape.

"Absolutely," he replied, a smile tugging at the corners of his lips. "It's time for us to explore what lies ahead, together." He took her hand, intertwining their fingers, grounding her amidst the swirling emotions of the moment.

They had decided to take a weekend trip to the nearby coastal town of Whitby—a place rich with history, breathtaking cliffs, and a spirit of adventure. It was a chance to escape the estate's haunting memories and to create new ones, unfettered by the shadows of their families' legacies.

As they made their way down the hill, the road ahead unfurling like a ribbon leading them toward the horizon, Elena felt the stirrings of anticipation. She could almost hear the call of the ocean, promising freedom and exploration. The journey felt symbolic, a physical manifestation of the emotional shift she had undergone in recent weeks.

With every step, they left behind the constraints of family expectations and the burdens of history, embracing the possibilities of their future together. The path ahead was bright, illuminated by the sun breaking through the clouds, casting a warm glow on the world around them.

When they arrived in Whitby, the salty breeze greeted them, carrying the sounds of seagulls and the gentle lap of waves against the shore. The town was vibrant, bustling with activity as locals and tourists mingled, all drawn to the charm of the seaside. Colorful storefronts lined the streets, inviting them to explore.

"Where to first?" Nathaniel asked, his eyes twinkling with excitement.

Elena grinned, feeling a sense of adventure bubbling within her. "Let's find a café by the sea. I want to feel the sand between my toes and taste the ocean air."

They strolled along the promenade, hand in hand, the golden sand glistening under the sun. With every step, Elena felt lighter, the remnants of her family's past fading further into the background. The weight of expectation, of obligation, was replaced by the sheer joy of discovery.

They settled at a quaint café overlooking the water, its outdoor seating adorned with vibrant flowers. As they sipped their coffee, the conversation flowed effortlessly, punctuated by laughter and shared dreams.

"What's next for you, aside from the mural?" Nathaniel asked, leaning back in his chair, a look of curiosity etched on his face.

"I've been thinking a lot about my art," Elena admitted, her gaze drifting toward the waves. "I want to start painting again—create pieces that reflect my journey, my family's legacy, and the beauty of the world around me. I want to tell our story through art, bridging the past and present."

"I'd love to see that," Nathaniel encouraged. "Your perspective is unique, and your voice deserves to be heard."

Elena smiled at his unwavering support, her heart swelling with gratitude. "Thank you for believing in me. I feel like I'm finally finding my way."

As the sun dipped lower in the sky, they wandered along the beach, collecting shells and stones, their laughter mingling with the sound of the waves. The horizon stretched before them, a canvas of colors blending into one another as day turned into night.

With the setting sun casting a golden hue over everything, Nathaniel paused, turning to Elena. "You know, we have a chance to create something beautiful together. Not just in art, but in our lives. It's a fresh start."

"Together," Elena echoed, her heart fluttering at the thought. The word felt powerful, carrying with it the promise of shared experiences, laughter, and love.

As they continued their stroll, they stumbled upon a rocky outcrop that jutted into the sea, a perfect spot to watch the sunset. Climbing carefully, they perched themselves on a ledge, the waves crashing below them.

Elena leaned into Nathaniel, feeling his warmth beside her as they watched the sun sink beneath the horizon, painting the sky in brilliant shades of orange, pink, and purple. "It's beautiful," she whispered, awe-struck by nature's splendor.

"Just like you," Nathaniel murmured, turning to her with a look that sent warmth coursing through her veins. "You've embraced the past and transformed it into something beautiful. I admire that strength."

Elena's cheeks flushed, and she looked away, embarrassed yet pleased. "I couldn't have done it without you. You helped me see the possibilities beyond the shadows."

He took her hand, his thumb brushing over her knuckles, and she felt the weight of his gaze on her. "And I want to continue to be by your side, exploring this journey together. Whatever the future holds, I want to face it with you."

With the last remnants of sunlight fading into twilight, Elena felt a surge of emotion. They had both weathered storms, faced their fears, and embraced the winds of change. Now, they stood on the cusp of something extraordinary, ready to explore the new horizons that awaited them.

"I want that too," she replied, her voice steady and resolute. "I want to create a life filled with love, art, and connection. With you, I feel like I can truly be myself."

They leaned closer, the world around them fading into the background, the crashing waves and gentle breeze becoming mere whispers in the presence of their shared intimacy. In that moment, as their lips met in a soft, tender kiss, Elena knew they were sealing their commitment to one another—a promise to embrace the journey ahead, no matter the challenges that lay in their path.

As they pulled away, their foreheads resting against each other, Elena felt a profound sense of peace. The winds of change had swept through their lives, carrying away the remnants of doubt and despair, leaving only hope and love in their wake.

Together, they would chart a course toward the future, hand in hand, hearts open to the adventures that awaited them. The shadows of the past had finally begun to dissipate, and in their place, a vibrant new chapter was unfolding—a journey fueled by love, courage, and the unwavering belief in the beauty of new beginnings.

29

The Calm After the Storm Serenity of the Heart

The morning sun streamed through the tall windows of Hawthorn Hill, casting warm beams of light across the grand foyer, illuminating the dust motes that danced in the air. Elena stood at the threshold of the estate, a brush in hand, ready to breathe life into the once-dreary walls that had witnessed so much sorrow. Now, however, they would become a sanctuary of joy—a testament to her family's transformation.

It had been weeks since their trip to Whitby, and the couple had returned with renewed spirits and a shared vision for the estate. Together, they had begun to restore Hawthorn Hill, infusing it with color and light, erasing the ghosts of its past. The weight of family legacy that once hung heavily over them had been lifted, replaced by the warmth of their love and the promise of new beginnings.

Elena glanced around at the canvases spread across the floor, each one filled with vibrant colors and bold strokes, echoing her journey of healing. Every brushstroke represented a piece of her heart, a piece of her family's history, now transformed into something beautiful. The once somber rooms were now alive with creativity, reflecting the happiness that had taken root in her soul.

"Are you ready for the big reveal?" Nathaniel's voice broke through her reverie, and she turned to find him standing in the doorway, a playful grin on his face. He held a palette of colors, ready to assist her in their artistic endeavors.

Elena laughed, her heart lifting at the sight of him. "As ready as I'll ever be! I can't wait to see your touch added to our masterpiece."

Nathaniel stepped into the room, placing the palette on the table as he approached her. "I've been thinking we should start with the library. It deserves to reflect the love and stories that live within its walls."

"Absolutely," Elena agreed, her eyes sparkling with excitement. "The library has always felt like the heart of this estate. It should be a place of inspiration, not just for us but for anyone who visits."

They spent the day painting and decorating, laughter echoing through the halls as they created together. Each stroke of the brush was a celebration of their love, a declaration that they had reclaimed Hawthorn Hill as their own. The walls transformed from muted grays and browns to soft pastels and rich hues, breathing life into the once-somber space.

As they painted, they shared stories of their hopes and dreams, their laughter mingling with the warm breeze that fluttered through the open windows. Nathaniel spoke of his artistic aspirations, of wanting to host art workshops for the community, while Elena shared her vision of inviting local artists to showcase their work in the estate.

"You know," Nathaniel said, pausing to admire their work, "I think we can create something beautiful here—a hub of creativity and inspiration that reflects the best of Hawthorn Hill. It could be a place where people come together to learn and grow."

"I love that idea," Elena replied, her heart swelling with joy at the thought of transforming their home into a beacon of creativity. "We can host events, art exhibits, even classes. We can turn this estate into a sanctuary for artists and dreamers."

As the sun began to set, casting a golden glow across the room, they stepped back to admire their handiwork. The library was now a sanctuary, filled with color and light, each corner inviting and warm. It felt like a space where stories would be written and shared—a place where new memories would be forged, far removed from the shadows of the past.

"Look at what we've created," Nathaniel said softly, taking Elena's hand. "This is just the beginning."

"Yes," she agreed, her voice tinged with emotion. "This is our beginning, a fresh start for both of us. I never imagined I could feel this free, this alive."

With the library transformed into a vibrant reflection of their love, they moved outside to the garden, where flowers were beginning to bloom in brilliant colors, the landscape thriving under their care. Elena had spent time cultivating the neglected grounds, planting new life amidst the remnants of the old. It was a labor of love, a promise to herself and to Nathaniel that they would nurture this place together.

They wandered through the blooming garden, hand in hand, breathing in the fragrant air. "I can't believe how far we've come," Nathaniel mused, gazing at the flowers swaying in the gentle breeze. "It feels like we've weathered the storm and found our peace."

Elena smiled, leaning into him. "It truly does. All those months of doubt and fear seem so far away now. I've finally found my voice, and it feels incredible."

As they reached the edge of the garden, where the view of the hills and valleys unfolded before them, Nathaniel turned to face Elena. The sun dipped lower in the sky, casting a warm glow around them. "I want to spend the rest of my life building this future with you. You've helped me find my purpose, and I can't imagine doing this with anyone else."

His words filled her with warmth and certainty. "I feel the same way. We've created something beautiful together, and I believe we can inspire others with our love and passion."

In that moment, under the fading sunlight and amidst the fragrant blooms, they sealed their commitment to one another with a kiss—a soft, tender affirmation of their shared dreams and aspirations. The kiss held the promise of a future untainted by the past, a commitment to nurture their love as they would the gardens surrounding them.

With the storms of Hawthorn Hill behind them, Elena and Nathaniel embraced the tranquility that followed, their hearts intertwined like the vines that climbed the estate's walls. They had transformed the estate into a sanctuary of joy, a place where love thrived and creativity blossomed, all rooted in their unwavering belief in one another.

As night fell and the stars began to twinkle in the vast sky, they returned to the library, where the flickering light of candles created a warm ambiance. Sitting side by side, they began to draft plans for their future—a future filled with art, love, and a community that celebrated the beauty of life.

And so, with the winds of change guiding them, Elena and Nathaniel began to chart their course, hand in hand, ready to embrace whatever came next. The calm after the storm had arrived, and in its embrace, they found serenity in their hearts, a love that would continue to flourish as they built their dreams together.

30

A Legacy of Love
The Eternal Bond

The first light of dawn broke over Hawthorn Hill, casting a soft glow that enveloped the estate in a golden embrace. Elena Hawthorne stood by the window of the library, gazing out at the expansive gardens that had blossomed into a riot of colors, a reflection of the life she had chosen with Nathaniel. Each petal, each leaf, seemed to whisper the story of their love—a tale woven with threads of hope, passion, and transformation.

Today marked a significant occasion; the couple had invited friends, family, and members of the community to celebrate the grand reopening of Hawthorn Hill as a creative sanctuary. The estate, once shrouded in secrets and sorrow, would now serve as a haven for artists and dreamers, a legacy that embodied the spirit of love and renewal.

As the sun climbed higher, Nathaniel entered the room, a radiant smile on his face. "Are you ready for today?" he asked, the excitement in his voice infectious. He moved to stand beside her, their shoulders touching as they shared the view of their transformed home.

"I can hardly believe it's finally here," Elena replied, her heart swelling with pride. "We've put so much love into this place. It's amazing to see our dreams come to life."

"Just think of all the lives we can touch," Nathaniel said, his gaze filled with determination. "This estate can be a source of inspiration, a place where people can come together to share their stories and create."

Elena nodded, her mind swirling with visions of the future. "We'll host workshops, exhibitions, and community events. We'll invite artists to come and share their talents—this can be a place of learning and collaboration."

As they prepared for their guests, the atmosphere in the estate buzzed with anticipation. The library, now filled with vibrant colors and eclectic artworks, stood ready to welcome everyone. Flowers adorned every table, their fragrances mingling in the air, creating an inviting and warm ambiance.

As the first guests began to arrive, Elena felt a flutter of nerves. She exchanged a reassuring glance with Nathaniel, who took her hand in his, grounding her amidst the swirling excitement. Together, they greeted their visitors, their hearts swelling with gratitude as they witnessed the joy their transformed home brought to others.

Throughout the afternoon, laughter and conversation filled the halls of Hawthorn Hill. Local artists showcased their work, sharing their stories and techniques, while attendees mingled, creating connections that mirrored the bonds Elena and Nathaniel had formed. The estate buzzed with life, a stark contrast to the desolate shadows it had once harbored.

As the sun began to set, casting a warm golden hue over the gathering, Nathaniel took the opportunity to speak to the crowd. He stood at the center of the library, Elena by his side, and looked out at the faces illuminated by the flickering candlelight.

"Thank you all for being here today," he began, his voice steady and sincere. "This estate has long been a part of our family's history, filled with stories both joyous and painful. But today, we celebrate a new chapter—a legacy of love and creativity that we hope will inspire generations to come."

Elena felt a rush of emotion as she listened to Nathaniel's words. He had always been her rock, and now he stood before their community, speaking from the heart about the vision they had nurtured together.

"Here at Hawthorn Hill," he continued, "we want to create a sanctuary for artists and dreamers alike—a place where everyone can express themselves, share their stories, and find inspiration in the beauty of life. We believe that art has the power to heal, to connect, and to bring joy."

The crowd erupted in applause, a wave of warmth enveloping them. Elena felt her heart swell with pride and love, knowing they were embarking on a journey that would ripple through time.

After Nathaniel finished speaking, he turned to Elena, his eyes shining with affection. "Together, we've transformed this estate, and together, we will nurture it as a home for creativity and love."

With the celebration continuing around them, Elena took a moment to reflect on the journey that had brought her to this point. She thought of the storms they had weathered, the secrets unearthed, and the love that had blossomed in the face of adversity. Hawthorn Hill was no longer just an ancestral home; it was a testament to their resilience, a canvas of their shared dreams.

As night fell, the guests gathered outside for a lantern release, a symbolic gesture to send their hopes and dreams into the sky. One by one, they lit their lanterns, each flickering flame representing a wish for the future. Elena and Nathaniel held their lantern tightly, sharing whispered dreams and aspirations before releasing it into the night.

"May this be the beginning of something beautiful," Nathaniel said, watching as their lantern floated into the starry sky. "May the winds of change always carry the promise of a brighter future."

Elena squeezed his hand, feeling the weight of their shared commitment. "And may our love be the foundation upon which this legacy stands."

As they stood together, watching the lanterns drift away, Elena felt a sense of peace settle over her. Their love had transcended the shadows of the past, transforming Hawthorn Hill into a beacon of hope and creativity.

In the years that followed, the estate flourished, becoming a cherished haven for artists and dreamers. Elena and Nathaniel continued to host workshops, exhibitions, and community events, fostering a sense of belonging and connection. They cultivated a legacy of love that echoed through the halls of Hawthorn Hill, a testament to their enduring bond.

As the seasons changed and time flowed on, Elena and Nathaniel built a life filled with laughter, art, and inspiration. They watched as the garden bloomed each spring, just as their love continued to grow, ever resilient against the winds of change.

And in the heart of Hawthorn Hill, the eternal bond they had forged remained steadfast, a guiding light that would always carry the promise of a brighter future—a legacy that would endure long after they were gone, echoing through the generations that would come to call the estate home.

In the end, Hawthorn Hill was not merely an estate but a testament to love's power—a sanctuary where creativity blossomed, and dreams took flight, forever carried on the winds of change.

181 Storms of Hawthorn Hill

ABOUT THE AUTHOR

Laura Lee is a passionate author and speaker, born and raised in a small town where the values of community and resilience were instilled in her from a young age. Her upbringing in a close-knit environment sparked her curiosity about the world and the human experience, shaping her desire to inspire others through the written word.

With a background in personal development, Laura has dedicated her life to exploring the intersections of courage, compassion, and authenticity. Her journey through fears and dreams has led her to uncover the transformative power of self-discovery and emotional resilience, themes that resonate deeply in her work.